THE LEGEND OF KING ARTHUR

RETOLD BY ROBIN LISTER

ILLUSTRATED BY ALAN BAKER

DOUBLEDAY
NEW YORK LONDON TORONTO SYDNEY AUCKLAND

PUBLISHED BY DOUBLEDAY
a division of Bantam Doubleday Dell Publishing Group, Inc.,
666 Fifth Avenue, New York, New York 10103

DOUBLEDAY
and the portrayal of an anchor with a dolphin
are trademarks of Doubleday, a division of
Bantam Doubleday Dell Publishing Group, Inc.

Library of Congress Cataloging-in-Publication Data

Lister, Robin.
The legend of King Arthur.
Summary: A retelling of fourteen tales from the legend
of King Arthur, beginning with the wizard Merlin and ending
with the departure of Arthur for the magical isle of Avalon.
1. Arthurian romances. [1. Arthur, King. 2. Knights
and knighthood—Folklore. 3. Folklore—England]
I. Baker, Alan, ill. II. Title.
PZ8.1.L69Le 1990   398.2'2'0942   88-36262
ISBN: 0-385-26369-4

Text copyright © 1988 by Robin Lister
Illustrations copyright © 1988 by Grisewood & Dempsey, Ltd.

CONTENTS

Merlin's Cave   5

Merlin and the Dragons   6

Magic and Murder   16

Tintagel   22

The Sword in the Stone   28

War and Love   36

Excalibur   44

The Fellowship of the Round Table   48

Lancelot, Guinevere and Elayne   56

Homecoming   68

The Holy Grail   76

The Vengeance of Gawain   84

The Day of Destiny   90

Merlin's Farewell   96

MERLIN'S CAVE

y name is Merlin, a name to conjure with; Merlin the wizard; Merlin, King Arthur's friend. I live deep in a cave, a limestone treasure-house of water, rock and time. I sit beside a stream among the snow-white columns, formed where slowly stalagmites and stalactites have met.

I sit where I have sat for centuries, sunk in soft cushions on my seat of stone. Like my books, which lie scattered about me, I am being slowly fossilized by the steady drip of time. Already my limbs are set in shining stone. My hair and beard have frosted hard. Even if I woke I could not move. For where is the ancient magic that might rescue me?

It has not always been so. Before I came to this cave, which has since become my prison, more than a thousand years ago, I lived in a world quite different from yours. Then there was war and suffering, love and happiness, as there is today, but it was a marvelous time of knights and adventures, magic and monsters too. It is a marvelous tale, the story of that time, the story of Uther Pendragon, of Arthur and Guinevere and Arthur's knights. Above all it is the story of Arthur, King Arthur of Camelot and the Fellowship of the Round Table, but it is my story too, for I, Merlin, helped to make it possible. Without Merlin, Arthur would never have been born.

MERLIN
AND THE DRAGONS

I t all began a long, long time ago. It was an evil time. The cruel Saxons had overrun half of Britain, and all the major cities were in their hands. Vortigern, the British King, had fled from them with his remaining followers to the mountains of North Wales.

They called Vortigern "the Fox," but "the Snake" would have been a better name. His path to the throne was cleared by poison, smoothed by bribery and ankle-deep in blood. It was Vortigern who had brought the Saxons to Britain in the first place. He had paid them to come and fight his battles for him and now they wanted the kingdom for themselves. Vortigern had no one to turn to. He ran to the mountains because there was nowhere else to go.

I was a boy then, just thirteen, living in the small town of Carmarthen in South Wales. My grandfather was the King of Carmarthen and my mother was a princess, but I had never seen her, for she entered the abbey of St. Peter's on the day that I was born. Since I knew nothing about my father, I might as well have been an orphan, and I was brought up in my grandfather's house where his young wife, Vivian, nursed me as her own. Their children, my uncles and aunts, were the same age as me and treated me as a brother.

Later I went to the abbey school. The monks were kind and scholarly and I was very happy there, but the most important things I learned were the things I learned at home. For my grandfather was a priest of the old religion who knew the secrets of nature and of night. He passed them on to me and, like him, I had the Sight. I could see into the future and call up the past. I learned to prophesy and to read minds. From the beginning this set me apart.

One summer afternoon, after school, I went to play football with my friends. It was not quite football as you know it now but, remember, this happened long ago. A small band of soldiers sat in the shade beneath the town walls, watching our game. They were strangers—we knew all the soldiers in Carmarthen by name—and I could see that they were Vortigern's men by the red dragons emblazoned on their tunics. No doubt they had come to try and rally support for him. But I was too young to fight, so their presence was no concern of mine. Or so I thought.

When our game ended, the King's men were still there. It was a warm evening, but I shivered when I realized that they were staring at me. One of them came up and took me by the arm. He looked like their captain.

"Are you Prince Merlin?" he asked. "The one they call Merlin the Bastard?"

"Yes, my name is Merlin. But no one calls me 'Bastard' here." As I spoke, I saw the look of triumph on his face.

"Then, Bastard, you must come with us. Vortigern wants to see you. He needs your help."

He was sneering at me, as if to say, How could a mere boy help a King? His companions sniggered and I began to feel uneasy. What did the old Fox really want me for?

The soldiers came with me to my grandfather's house while I gathered together the few things I needed: my heavy cloak, my boots and the ancient gold bracelet my mother had left me. Then I tiptoed into my grandfather's room. He lay on his bed, staring into space as he had done for months now, waiting to die. His dim blue eyes turned toward me and he stretched out a trembling, bloodless hand.

"Merlin, dearest boy," he whispered, "this is the last time you will see me alive. Be careful, for Vortigern is treacherous and cruel, but don't be afraid. When I die all my magic powers will be yours and I have only a few days left to live. It is God's will."

Tears streamed down my face as I said goodbye. I knew that I was kissing him for the last time. Outside, Vortigern's men were waiting with my horse. There was another rider with them, a slight figure in a black veil, but I was thinking too much about what my grandfather had said to wonder who it might be.

The journey took four days. We hurried north through the high passes, riding hard from dawn till dusk. Each day the sun shone and I gazed in wonder at the wild beauty of the country. I noticed that we avoided the settlements and small forts along our route. My guards were nervous and I could sense their fear each time we saw someone ahead of us on the road.

On the last night of our journey, we made our camp beneath a clear moonlit sky. We all looked up and gasped: the bright yellow moon was slowly disappearing before our eyes. After half an hour it had gone, leaving only the faintest glow behind. My guards threw themselves to the ground, covering their heads, while our veiled companion knelt in silent prayer. But I continued to look up, remembering the astronomy my grandfather had taught me, and just as I expected, after a pause, the moon slowly reappeared. My guards struggled to their feet, shaken and subdued. The world had not ended after all, but I think the message was clear, even to them. Vortigern's light was not merely on the wane, it was fading fast.

Next morning we had not ridden far before the great mountains of Snowdonia came into view. Vortigern's camp lay on the banks of a small river in the valley below Mount Snowdon itself. Long before we reached the camp I could see the half-built castle of Dinas Emrys on the foothill above. The desperate King was trying to build an impregnable fortress, even though he had no country left to defend.

The camp was unguarded. A handful of sick and injured men lay among makeshift tents. Everywhere women were hard at work, cooking, mending and washing in the stream. Bands of wild-looking children ran about as they pleased. We climbed the slope, past a trail of weary horses dragging cartloads of heavy stone.

From a distance the building had looked quite small. But when we saw it close to at the top of the hill, I realized that it covered an area larger than Carmarthen. But it was not its size which surprised me most, it was the chaos of the site. Everywhere I looked, unfinished walls had cracked and crumbled, while Vortigern's flag, showing a red dragon, drooped from the ruins of a tower. The King himself stood among a group of priests and ministers, looking disconsolate, while men scurried everywhere, trying to clear away the ruined masonry.

At the first shout of "They're back," everyone stopped what they were doing. I was pulled from my horse and bundled toward the King, my veiled companion beside me. A crowd quickly gathered around us, jostling to see who we were.

"These are the ones you asked for, my lord. The Bastard and the nun."

Impatiently, Vortigern waved the captain away. Beside him stood a man in a white cowl, who lunged toward me. Vortigern held him back.

"Patience, Maugantius, patience."

Then the King stepped forward, rings glinting in the sun as he squeezed my chin and peered into my eyes.

"So you are Merlin. Yes, yes, just like the old man." He waved an arm around the ruins. "You are welcome to my palace."

I rubbed my bruised chin as he turned to my companion.

"Dear Princess, you are welcome too. I must apologize for forcing you to come, but this is a matter of the utmost importance and there are questions which only you can answer. It won't take long. Then my men will take you back at once. Maugantius, please."

Maugantius had been staring at me while Vortigern spoke. Now he turned to the mysterious figure beside me.

"Princess, you have taken the vow of silence, I know. But God will forgive you if you break it now. I have just two simple questions to ask you. Is this boy your son? And, if he is, then who is his father?"

"Yes, Merlin is my son." The words came in a whisper. It was the first time I had heard my mother's voice. Then she turned toward me, lifting her veil to show her pale, drawn face. "Oh, Merlin, Merlin, you have no human father. It was a false devil who came to me in my dreams."

Vortigern was unable to hide his excitement. "Maugantius, can what she says be true?"

"Certainly, my lord. The wise have written of such things. A thousand spirits, half-angel and half-man, live between the earth and the moon. It is clearly one of these that visited the princess. Merlin is fatherless, just as we had hoped."

The guards tightened their grip on my arms as Maugantius pulled a dagger from the folds of his cowl.

"My lord," he hissed, "give me the word."

My head was swimming and I could feel my knees buckle beneath me. The peering, hostile faces surrounding me spun around. I knew that if I fainted that would be the end, so I closed my eyes and clung to my mind, like a drowning man clings to a plank. I managed to hold on.

I opened my eyes to find that I was being dragged toward a marble slab in the middle of the site. Squirming free of the guards, I leaped onto the slab and raised my arms. The mob stopped in its tracks.

"What superstitious rite is this?" I shouted. "What murderous sacrifice? I challenge you, Maugantius, to say why I must die."

"Don't listen to him, my lord," Maugantius snarled. "Even the minutes are precious. The boy must die at once."

But once more Vortigern held him back. "No, Merlin is right. He shall be told." The old Fox smiled at me. "You see the ruins of our castle here. This is the second time it has collapsed. Yet the foundations are built on solid rock and my master masons are the best there are. Maugantius told me why. It seems that this is sacred ground. The spirit of the mountains is angry and only a blood sacrifice will appease it. If the foundations are sprinkled with the blood of a fatherless boy, they will stand firm. Merlin, we know now that you are that boy."

"This is not ancient magic, Vortigern," I replied. "These are black lies. The Egyptians used the blood of orphans in this way, to please their cruel gods. The Romans did the same. But it won't work here. You could drench your foundations in the blood of a thousand Merlins and your walls would crumble just the same."

"Insolent whelp!" Maugantius leapt toward me, raising his knife above his head. Vortigern seized his arm.

"Wait. Let the boy speak." He turned back to me, his smile gone. "Well, boy, go on then. Tell me what all my great wise men could not."

I closed my eyes. A picture came into my mind.

"I see a sealed cavern underground, filled by a deep pool. At the bottom of the pool lie two hollow stones. In each of the stones a dragon is sleeping, one white, one red."

I opened my eyes to look at my audience, who stood quite still now, waiting to hear what I would say.

"Your foundations aren't built on rock, Vortigern. They lie on a thin crust of earth, covering a pool. You must drain the pool and fill it in. Then your walls will stand."

Maugantius tried to speak, but Vortigern ignored him. He called his chief mason over.

"I want your best men. The boy can show them where to work. Now, Merlin, let's see this pool."

I led the men through the ruins to an area which had already been cleared. Then I set them to work. As they pounded the earth with their picks and hammers, hollow cracks and thuds rang across the valley. But

soon we heard a different sound. A shout went up. The men had broken through.

We all crowded around the opening, and saw our own faces staring back at us from the dark surface of the water. Then the masons took over. They brought up pumps and started to drain the pool while the rest of us waited in silence. Even great Vortigern had been struck dumb and I noticed that Maugantius had gone.

We waited and waited until the pool was drained. Then we peered nervously into the hole. Two oblong stones lay side by side on the muddy bottom. They looked like tombs, big enough to hold ten men. Strange muffled sounds came from inside them. Then they started to crack and sharp claws and scaly limbs appeared. The crowd drew back in horror while I alone remained where I stood at the edge of the pool.

Within moments two dragons had climbed out beside me. One was red, the other white. They were breathing fire in short bursts of flame which sizzled on the wet earth. Ignoring me, the dragons began to fight, tearing at each other's shiny skin and panting fierce balls of flame. In turn, they forced each other back toward the hole.

I turned to Vortigern, who was cowering behind a pile of stones.

"Alas for the Red Dragon, Vortigern, for its end is near. The White Dragon will overrun its lairs and cavernous dens. The rivers and streams will run with blood and the mountains will groan for the suffering people. The country will cry out in pain. Finally a boar will come to end the strife and bring a time of peace. Then Britain will rejoice and cry out for joy. You are the Red Dragon, Vortigern. The boar's name is Arthur."

I came out of my prophetic trance to see the end of the fight. The White Dragon had the Red Dragon down and was ripping at its throat. The dying dragon's tail thrashed wildly in the mud until, with a mighty roar, the White Dragon heaved it over the edge. It crashed down into the dregs of the pool, shuddered horribly and lay still. With another triumphant roar, the White Dragon spread its vast wings, beat them and slowly floated up above us. It circled the mountain, breathing flame, then wheeled away toward the sun. We watched it go, until the glittering creature had dwindled to a speck.

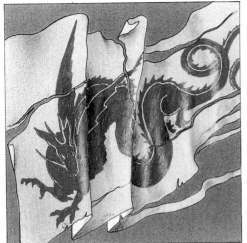

Only then did Vortigern and his followers creep out from behind the stones where they had been hiding. As they did so, Vortigern's flag, with its proud red dragon, fell from the ruined tower and lay crumpled in the mud.

Vortigern clutched at my sleeve.

"For God's sake, Merlin, tell me what to do."

I shook off his hand. He was doomed and there was nothing I could do. But although he had been prepared to kill me to save his own life, I felt sorry for him now.

"The best thing you can do is run," I said. "Run to the coast and keep on running. For even as we speak, Aurelius and Uther are leading a great army from the south. You murdered their father and brother and stole their kingdom, and you would have killed them too if they had not escaped to Brittany. The young princes are now men and they are coming for revenge."

Vortigern turned pale.

"Where can I run to, Merlin? To the east are the Saxons. To the west the sea. I have no ships; and worse still, I have no friends."

"Then I suggest you build your fortress here, as quickly as you can. Fill in the hole and build strong walls. Your enemies will have to starve you out. If you can hold them off till winter, who knows?"

Anyone could see that it would take months to rebuild those walls. But Vortigern was desperate, and I left him there, among the ruins, bullying his exhausted men.

My mother was praying, her head bowed. Taking her hand, I led her down the hill. We found our horses, which had bolted from the dragons, wandering nervously among the tents. We rode out the way we had come. Shouts and bangs echoed behind us, growing fainter as we climbed up out of the valley.

We stuck to the difficult high passes because I was anxious to avoid being seen. We rode for three days, stopping each night to rest. Then we talked and my mother told me many things, about her own childhood and her life in the abbey. She questioned me closely too. She spoke tenderly, this mother I had never had, and I often saw tears glistening in her eyes.

On the fourth day the first part of my prophecy was confirmed. We were making our way along a ridge when we heard a deep murmuring in the distance, ahead of us. We reined in our horses and sheltered behind some rocks. Before long the sound of marching feet and hooves grew louder and the first banners came into view. Soon the valley below was filled with men and horses. Everywhere their banners, emblazoned with white dragons, proclaimed who they were. Aurelius and Uther had arrived.

We reached Carmarthen by nightfall to find the gates open and the ramparts deserted. I escorted my mother back to the abbey before making my way to my grandfather's house.

It was surrounded by blazing torches. A crowd had gathered outside it, talking in low voices. When the people saw me, they fell silent and stood back to let me pass. His body was laid out where I had left him, only now it was covered in flowers and encircled by candles. I knelt by the bed and took his cold hands in mine. My grandfather was dead and his last words to me had already been proved true. I had inherited his magic powers. I prayed, as I knelt beside him, that I would use them well.

MAGIC AND MURDER

Time passed. Vortigern was burned alive in his half-built castle and no one shed a tear. Aurelius took his rightful crown and the long-suffering British people flocked to his side. The Saxon army was heavily defeated in a pitched battle outside York and its treacherous leader, Hengist, was captured and beheaded. When his son, Octa, surrendered and swore an oath of loyalty to Aurelius, it seemed that at long last the years of bloodshed and suffering were over. Britain was at peace.

Carmarthen was still mourning my grandfather's death when the news of all these victories reached the town. Suddenly sadness turned to triumph but I took no part in the celebrations, for I missed the old man bitterly. Compared to losing him, Vortigern's death and Aurelius' glory seemed unimportant and far away. Of my visit to Vortigern, of the pool and the dragons, and of my visions and prophecies, I said nothing. I had the Sight, but I was young and inexperienced, so I watched and waited, knowing my time would come. As the months went by, I came to terms with my grief and the years that followed were happy ones for me. I continued my studies at the abbey school, and life in Carmarthen went on slowly and peacefully, as it had always done. Away from my books I still spent my time with my friends, hunting deer and boar in the old forests of Carmarthenshire, learning to use swords, and flirting with the girls. We considered ourselves too old for football now.

Meanwhile, I dreamed my magic dreams and turned to my secret studies with a new intensity, just as I knew my grandfather would have wished. The old man had left me all his ancient books and charts, which I pored over, night after sleepless night, by moon and candlelight. I would shut myself away at the top of the tower overlooking the royal house. As far back as I could remember, this had been "Merlin's room," while the rest of the family slept together in the main part of the house.

This arrangement suited me well. I loved my little room, where I felt as if I sat among the stars, which held the mysteries of the universe. And there was still so much to learn.

The things I studied were called "magic" in those days. In your brave modern world, you call them "science." I learned about optics and built a telescope to see things far away. I made a microscope to see what was invisible to the naked eye. I understood the principles of gravity, space and time and I learned about the chemistry of life. Here was magic, indeed! I mapped out the movements of the constellations, their tiniest shifts, their largest sweeps. I saw the future and realized that I could help to shape it. I could move mountains if I was called upon to do it. It seemed there was nothing that I could not do. For the moment, however, I knew that I must prepare myself, for my real task still lay ahead of me. I would do many things, but I knew that one day I would make a King who would become the greatest King that ever lived. The image of his face was already there, in my mind's eye.

The years passed and I grew into a man. An air of mystery surrounded me, for secrets were hard to keep in a small town like ours and, in spite of my own silence on the matter, the story of the boy and the dragons had grown into a legend. Besides, people saw the candle in my tower, burning through the night. Naturally, they wondered what I was up to.

When, at last, the call came, I was ready for it, but when I saw the messenger's face, I had to rub my eyes. It was the captain who had taken me to Vortigern at Dinas Emrys ten years before. He wore a white dragon now, emblazoned on his tunic where the red dragon had been.

"My lord Aurelius has sent for you, noble Merlin." He smiled at me as though we were old friends.

"Don't you mean 'Bastard'?" I asked him coldly.

He paled. "Don't hold it against me," he stammered. "I was only following orders. We're all on the same side now."

It was true. Over the months which followed I recognized a number of Vortigern's men in the service of Aurelius. But there was one face I did not see until it was too late.

The captain and his soldiers now led me to London and this time the journey was uneventful. My escort was relaxed and cheerful and there were signs of a new prosperity everywhere. It came as a shock when we passed the untouched remains of a burned-out village, a grim reminder of the recent past. Now the harvests were abundant, the livestock well fed and the people happy. How different it had been just ten short years ago . . .

The royal court at Westminster was even more splendid than I had imagined. A noble palace stretched out beside the Thames, next to the abbey church. Even the guards wore finer clothes than the princes of Carmarthen. As for the lords and ladies, their colourful silks and rich gold braids dazzled my innocent eyes.

King Aurelius was just as I had pictured him: strong and handsome with an intelligent face, so like the face of the future King which I carried in my mind. His brother, Uther, looked like him, although younger, but I quickly learned how different they were. Aurelius was proud, remote and single-minded to a fault. The people respected him, but he was not loved. I could never have got as close to him as I did to Uther, who was hot-blooded and passionate by nature, and warm and loving too.

However, Aurelius welcomed me kindly, and I was made much of at the court. At first I had little to do so I attended sessions of the King's Council and saw at first hand how government worked. The Chancellor, Gorlois, Duke of Cornwall, was an old acquaintance of mine who had visited Carmarthen several times. At the palace, as at home, I was given a room at the top of a tower. I had brought all my books and instruments with me— they had filled an entire wagon—and, since I no longer slept, I was able to continue my nocturnal studies. Early one morning, I heard the door open and I looked up from my calculations to see Aurelius standing there.

"So, Merlin, what they say is true: you live without sleep. Here, come into the light."

Getting up from my chair, I stepped toward him and he held his candle to my face.

"I knew your grandfather. He visited me once in Brittany. You've got his face, all right, and they tell me that you've also got the Sight."

"My lord, I know a little," I replied. "But I'm still young."

"From what I see you know enough," answered Aurelius. "The thing is, are you with us? Will you put your powers to good use?"

"I'm with you, my lord."

"Merlin, my end is near. No, don't lie to me like the others. I know how to read my dreams. I can almost feel the poison in my veins. I will die soon and I want to leave something great behind. Some great monument, some magic building that will last forever."

He walked to my window and stared out to the west, away from the dawn.

"Can you do it, Merlin?" he asked without looking around. "Will you do it for me?"

"Yes, my lord, I can."

I had been planning it since my arrival in London.

I took Uther and two hundred men. We reached Ireland in ten days. We arrived at night, sailing upriver to our destination without being seen. We had come for the Giant's Ring, an ancient stone circle full of magic and sacred to the Irish race. When the men saw it, they laughed in disbelief. How, they asked me, could a mere two hundred move the smallest of these stones? It had taken tens of thousands to build the Egyptian pyramids.

I showed them how. First we made levers and cranes, then we rolled away the great stones and loaded them onto our ships. No one disturbed us, although there was a town nearby. We had all the time we needed, for that night I made time stand still.

We shipped the stones back to Britain, levered them onto a moving road of logs and rolled them to Salisbury Plain. I cannot say if Stonehenge will last forever—I am not God—but the magic ring of stones still stands today.

Poor, proud Aurelius never saw his monument. That night we made our camp beside Stonehenge. While the others slept, I wandered among the standing stones, which were bathed in silver moonlight, breathing in the magic power of the place. Suddenly a shooting star burst into brilliant light and sped across the sky. It left a trail of fire in the shape of a dragon. Then, as I watched, the dragon became a boar. The vision had scarcely faded when another star appeared. Once more the blazing signs were spread across the sky. Then a third star came; the vision was still more brilliant than before. I rushed over to Uther and shook him awake.

"We must go at once," I cried. "Aurelius is dead."

As we rode east, into the dawn, I explained what I had seen. The star was Aurelius, whose fire had gone out. Uther was the dragon that took his place. The boar who followed would be Arthur, the boar of Cornwall, Uther's future son.

We arrived two days later to find the court in turmoil. Aurelius had died two nights before. Now there were reports of a great army coming from the north, destroying everything in its path. Hengist's son, Octa, the Saxon leader, together with Vortigern's son, Paschent, had raised a rebellion.

"Thank heaven you're here," said Gorlois, whose gray hair had turned white overnight. Dark shadows ringed his eyes. "He died so suddenly, just when we thought the monk had cured him."

"The monk?" I asked sharply.

"Yes, Eopa."

"Where is he?" I grabbed Gorlois by the shoulders.

"He's been in the chapel, praying, ever since."

"Come on, Uther, quick."

We ran to the chapel. There was no one there, but I could sense his presence. Pretending to leave, I led Uther to the door, opened it and slammed it shut. We stood in the shadows, waiting. A dry cough came from the bell tower.

Quickly, we crept up the winding stairs and took the stranger by surprise. His face was half hidden beneath his cowl, but there was something familiar about him. He told us that Paschent had sent him and that the rebel army would attack that very evening. As he spoke, he looked out from the tower toward the north, and our eyes followed his gaze, half expecting to see a great army in the distance. In that instant he sprang out of reach. A blade flashed out from his white cloak as he circled around us, making for the stairs.

"Everything worked," he hissed, "but you came back a day too soon. You spoiled my plans once before, Merlin, when your cheap magic fooled the mad old King. But you won't get another chance."

I was waiting for the lunge and I stepped aside. The thrust, aimed at my heart, passed harmlessly by, but the momentum carried my assailant forward. He stumbled, collided with the great church bell and crashed through the opening beneath it. The stone floor was fifty feet below. We waited for the sickening thud, but instead there was a sharp jerk on the bell rope, followed by a discordant peal.

Risking our own necks on the narrow steps, we rushed down after him, but we need not have worried. Now he would never get away. His cowl had become entangled in the rope as he fell, catching around his neck, and his lifeless body dangled in the air, swinging from side to side. Up above, the bell slowly tolled. I helped Uther cut the body down. The face was just the same. Eopa was Maugantius.

It was easy to guess who else was involved in the plot. Vortigern's old captain was quick to confess that Maugantius had threatened him until he promised to help. His task was to unbolt the gates at nightfall. Then a peal of the bell would give the signal for the rebels to attack.

We set a trap and waited for dusk. When we rang the bell, the rebel army poured in through the gates. Our arrows rained down on them from every side and it was all over within an hour. No prisoners were taken.

The next day Uther was crowned King. He had a golden dragon made, in memory of my vision. The people called him Uther Pendragon, Uther Dragonhead, from that day on.

Tintagel

The new King's first task was to restore peace. Octa and Paschent's rebellion had left a trail of terror and destruction across the country, while in the wild far north, no one was safe from Scottish border raids.

Uther threw himself into these new campaigns with a will. He was an inspired general and before long his enemies were defeated. But now the King and his army were continually on the move. He spent less and less time at Westminster, not daring to leave his powerful subjects to their own devices for long, particularly in the north. Besides, a soldier's life suited him. Uther was easily bored by the polite ceremonies of court life; he despised soft comforts and thrived on constant change. When there was no fighting to be done, he held tournaments up and down the country, proving himself a great champion, in sport as in war.

Ten years went by, during which time I was always at Uther's side. I was his chief adviser from the beginning, for our Irish adventure and the events surrounding his brother's death had made us fast friends. Then, after ten years, I decided the time had come. I told Uther that although he was still vigorous and young, he must think about the future. It was time to take a wife. I didn't tell him that I had a prophecy to fulfil. Uther agreed and, on my advice, he called a marriage council of all the great British lords.

They were to assemble at Westminster at Christmas to help him make his choice. If Uther's marriage was to bring harmony, not strife, it was important that a majority approved it. This was true, of course. But I had another, quite different motive, as you will see.

After the death of Aurelius, white-haired Gorlois, Chancellor of Britain and Duke of Cornwall, had returned to his dukedom. He was tired of the court and he had decided to retire before he was too old to enjoy an active life. In particular, he wanted to spend more time with his beautiful young wife, Igrayne.

I had seen Igrayne in my dreams. She was the loveliest woman in Britain and I knew exactly what would happen when Uther saw her.

Gorlois and Igrayne arrived at Westminster on the appointed day. The old duke sat in council. The lords and bishops discussed this King's daughter and that earl's sister, but Uther was not listening. He had just seen the only woman he wanted to marry. Unfortunately, she was already married to his oldest and most loyal follower. Poor Gorlois, he could not bear to see how Uther looked at Igrayne; still less to see how she looked back. Against all the age-old laws of hospitality and friendship, of loyalty and duty to his King, he took his wife, left London secretly by night and fled straight back to Cornwall.

Uther pretended to be furious, but the old duke's behavior gave him just the excuse he wanted. He announced that Gorlois had defied him and that unless he returned at once, with Igrayne, to make a full apology, he would be treated as a traitor.

Poor, loyal Gorlois. Was this his reward for all those years of service to the crown? He secured Igrayne in Tintagel Castle, and waited for Uther at Dimilioc nearby. He reasoned that if he stayed in Tintagel with Igrayne, then Uther could starve them out. But if he, Gorlois, were elsewhere, then Uther would have to attack him. He would probably die, but surely Uther's remorse would protect Igrayne from his lust. He did not know his man.

The siege of Dimilioc Castle was barely a week old when Uther took me to one side.

"Merlin, I can't wait any longer. I must be with Igrayne this very night, or I'll go mad."

"But Igrayne's not here, Uther. She's at Tintagel. You know as well as anyone that three soldiers could defend that place against an entire army. Nevertheless, if you grant me a promise, then perhaps there's a way."

Uther smiled. "What's this, Merlin, must I pay for your services now?"

"Yes, my most noble lord," I replied, making a mock bow. "But it's a small thing that I ask."

"Go on, my good wizard, ask away."

"You will be with Igrayne tonight, my lord. And tonight, by you, she will conceive a son. But you must promise me this: when that child is one year old, you will let me take him away and look after him. I will educate him. I will prepare him for kingship. You won't see him again. But he will succeed you. And he will be the greatest King Britain has ever had."

"Merlin, Merlin, anything you like. Just get me to Igrayne."

Uther had spoken. My dream was in my grasp.

It was a moonless night. The wind howled and the icy rain lashed down. Three figures on horseback rode out across the headland to Tintagel. As they approached the narrow bridge at the cliff's edge, a voice barked out nervously through the night.

"Get off your horses. And keep still, or you're dead."

The riders dismounted and patted their frightened horses to calm them. They could see the archers silhouetted against the sky. Three arrows pointed at each of their pounding hearts.

At last torches appeared on the far side of the bridge. They flickered and sputtered in the wind and rain, jerking up and down as they moved forward through the night.

"Hurry up down there," the voice barked out again. It was tense and impatient now.

The torches jerked across the bridge and closed in on the new arrivals. The guards held them up to their faces.

"Gorlois!" gasped the captain. His voice showed his relief. "Guards, lower your weapons." He turned back to the horsemen. "My lord, forgive this suspicious welcome. We weren't expecting friends. I thought you were at Dimilioc."

"So I was, so I was," replied the stooping figure. His white hair shone in the torchlight. "But the siege looks set in for months. I decided to slip away for one night. I wanted to be sure all was well here."

Behind his back the guards exchanged knowing looks with the duke's two companions, Brastias and Jordan. They winked back at the guards. All the King's horses and all the King's men had not kept the old man away.

The three men led their horses across the swaying bridge. Torches lit their way. Under their feet the sea boiled and heaved. Huge breakers climbed the cliffs and crashed back down. Then they were across and the castle gates clanged shut behind them.

Igrayne received her husband dutifully. She pretended that she was pleased to see him, although she much preferred to be alone. Her thoughts were all of Uther now.

By morning the storm had passed. Deep snow covered the ground. As they left, the three riders turned back to gaze at the magical castle on the whitened rock, surrounded by sea. It shone in the watery sunlight.

They did not see the figure in the tower, staring out after them. Igrayne was puzzled. Gorlois had looked the same. But he had not been as she remembered him.

The riders wheeled away and galloped back over the headland toward Dimilioc. Whooping in boyish triumph, their leader burst into song. Igrayne would not have recognized her husband now, for this was Uther Pendragon riding out from Tintagel.

I, Merlin, rode beside him and Sir Ulfius, one of Uther's knights, rode with us. We no longer needed our disguises. We reached Dimilioc to find that the siege was over. Gorlois, anxious about Igrayne, had tried to slip past the royal army during the night but he and his companions had been spotted and challenged by the royal guard. Instead of surrendering, they attempted to escape. Poor Gorlois had been killed.

Igrayne told me much later that she fainted when she heard the news. She had realized at once that by the time we reached Tintagel that night, Gorlois was already dead.

As for me, I did not whoop or sing. But deep in my heart I rejoiced.

THE SWORD IN THE STONE

Nine months later, far away in London, Arthur entered the world. By this time Igrayne was Uther's Queen; she had not mourned Gorlois for long.

The royal wedding had been a grand occasion. All the nobility of Britain and France was there. Besides Uther and Igrayne, two of the new Queen's daughters were married on the same day. Morgause married King Lot of Lothian and Orkney, while Elayne married King Nentres of Garlot. Uther now had two powerful sons-in-law.

But Igrayne's youngest daughter and the one she loved most, Morgan le Fay, stayed away. Morgan had loved her old father, Gorlois, and she blamed me for his death. She hated Uther too and cursed the unborn child. I had not foreseen this, but even if I had, it would have changed nothing. Nevertheless, I was worried: like me, Morgan had the Sight, and I could not ignore her curse.

The last year with Uther was a painful one for me. Igrayne liked me, and Uther himself was as affectionate as ever, but they both doted on Morgan, whose charm was irresistible, and Morgan was determined to come between us. She even tried to keep me from the child. She pretended to adore her baby brother and treated her royal stepfather with such respect that no one would have believed that she hated them both from the bottom of her heart. No one except me. I knew she was biding her time, waiting for revenge.

I watched and waited until the year was out. The appointed day came at last, and I packed my books and instruments and took the baby in my arms. Igrayne pleaded with me until the tears streamed down her face. Uther avoided my eyes.

"Go quickly, old friend," he whispered, "before I change my mind."

Morgan was taken by surprise. She had not known about Uther's promise and now it was too late to stop me.

28

I took Arthur back to Carmarthen, where I was given a hero's welcome by my uncle Dinabutius, who had become King when my grandfather died. The whole town came out to greet me. Later, I stayed at my grandfather's old house and talked and laughed about old times, but I said nothing about the child sleeping peacefully among my books.

That night I smuggled the baby into my room and early the next morning, while everyone slept, I strapped him to my back and rode out to Sir Hector's. Hector, who had been a childhood friend, was a good, old-fashioned country knight, living on his family estate a few miles outside the town. He and his wife welcomed me, and made much of little Arthur. I told them he was an orphan, a foundling I had taken pity on, and they agreed to take him in and raise him as their own with their son, Kay, who was five years old. That night, as I rode back to Carmarthen alone, I finally felt at peace. Deep in South Wales, Morgan's curse seemed far away.

The months passed and I soon felt as though I had never been away. The royal house was full of children now and I quickly became their favorite uncle: Uncle Merlin, the King of Britain's friend, who knew a thousand stories of magic and adventure.

Then, two years after I left the court, Morgan took her revenge: Uther died suddenly of unknown causes. I knew it was her. I knew it as clearly as you see this page. When I heard the news, I shut myself in my tower. My first thoughts were of vengeance, but I quickly calmed myself, realizing that it was useless to struggle against destiny. Besides, there was much to be done before another, far greater destiny than Uther's could be fulfilled.

I visited Arthur every week. He was a healthy, happy child. When he was four, he came to the abbey school with his brother, Kay. During the week they stayed in the royal house, for Hector and Dinabutius were old friends. At weekends and holidays they returned to the family home.

The monks took care of Arthur's formal education, while I taught him who he was and where he came from. I told him about my grandfather, Vortigern, the dragons, Aurelius, Uther and Igrayne. For some reason I never told him about Morgan; he learned about her much later. I cannot decide, looking back, whether this was a mistake. Perhaps it would have made a difference, after all.

Meanwhile, in Britain, troubled times returned. Igrayne ruled, but she was a puppet Queen. Civil war loomed as powerful lords disputed Uther's crown and the specter of bloodshed and famine haunted the country once more. Only in a backwater like Carmarthen could life go on unchanged.

The years went by and Arthur grew with them. By the age of ten, he looked so much like Uther that I expected the rumors to fly. But Carmarthen was a sleepy place and the few who had known the late King, such as Dinabutius, had always seen him with a beard.

As I said, Arthur was quick to learn. He was strong and daring too. By the age of fifteen, he could outrun, outthrow and outjump the whole of Carmarthenshire. But he was careful never to beat his brother Kay, a proud young squire of twenty who was anxious to go to the next great tournament in London to be knighted and prove his worth. For the sake of Kay's pride and peace at home, Arthur always let him win. He was more than a scholar and athlete. He was already a diplomat, wise beyond his years.

When he was sixteen, I decided that he was ready. I would have preferred to wait another five years, but it might have been too late, for the country was torn apart by fighting and even Carmarthenshire was threatened now. I left for London alone. The road was no longer safe for unprotected travelers, but I could take care of myself if the need arose. The invisible horseman fears no thieves.

Igrayne made me welcome and was overjoyed to have news of her long-lost son. As for me, I was glad to learn that Morgan was far away in France. Soon after Uther's death she had married Uriens, King of Gore. I prayed she would leave us in peace.

The situation in Britain had become so desperate that Igrayne and her ministers fell in with my plan at once. They were grateful for any help they could get, and here was the famous Merlin, come to save them. Following my instructions, it was decreed that all the great lords and knights of the realm would be called to the Palace of Westminster at Christmas to choose a new King. Everyone had to attend; those who stayed away would be denounced as traitors.

The weeks went by and the first arrivals started to trickle in. By Christmas Day every lodging house in London was full and the servants were forced to camp out where they could, despite the bitter cold. There had not been a gathering like this since the great tournaments of Uther's time. Hundreds of lords and ladies crowded into the abbey, while thousands of commoners thronged outside, pressing up against the doors. The Archbishop of Canterbury led the service, and we prayed to God for guidance.

Nobody could explain how it got there, although some of you might guess (it was a simple matter, compared to the Giant's Ring). The congregation left the church to find a block of marble standing in the middle of the churchyard. A steel anvil holding a beautiful sword was set into the block. In bold gold letters on each side of the block an inscription had been carved into the stone:

Scuffles broke out among the lords. Each of them thought he should be first in the queue. But their fighting spirit was soon dampened when it turned out that not one of them could budge the sword, not even the merest fraction of an inch. The crowd grew angry, feeling they had been cheated.

I leaped up onto the stone and addressed them.

"The time has not yet come, but believe me, the time is near. Good lords, be patient. Wait for the great tournament at New Year. After the tournament you can try the sword again."

The great tournament was held in Westminster fields, by the river. There had not been an occasion like it for many years. The fields were a mass of color and excitement, and no one was more excited than the two young men of Carmarthenshire who had come with their father.

The father and the younger boy were getting the older one ready. Besides his solid breastplate and helmet, he was covered in chain mail from head to toe. Together they hoisted him into the saddle. His powerful charger snorted and bared its teeth.

"Now for the sword, Kay," said Sir Hector. He looked across the fields. "Come on, the next joust's about to start."

"The sword, where's my sword?" cried Kay, impatiently.

The younger boy put his hand to his mouth. His cheeks had turned bright red.

"Oh, Arthur, you idiot. You haven't left it behind, have you?"

Their father burst out laughing.

"Calm down, Kay. It won't make any difference if you miss a joust or two. Arthur can go back and fetch your sword."

Arthur rushed back to their lodgings but, to his dismay, he found the house locked and barred. Their landlady had already left. He would never find her in the crowd.

Arthur felt desperate. Without a sword Kay could not enter the lists, and it was all his fault. He was about to go back when he remembered the sword in the stone which he had glimpsed in the churchyard the day before. There had not been time to read the inscription.

"I'll borrow that sword, if it's still there," he told himself. "Kay can use it today and I'll put it back this evening. Even the monks and priests are at the tournament, so no one will miss it."

Just as he thought, there was no one there. Arthur looked at the marble. To his surprise, the inscription had disappeared. Perhaps he had imagined it. Effortlessly, he pulled the sword out of the stone and rushed back to the fields. Without a word of thanks, Kay grabbed the sword and turned to go over to the lists. Then he realized that this was not his sword. He looked at it carefully and began to tremble. He had seen this sword before and he had read the words beneath it.

"Father, father," he cried breathlessly. "Look, this is the sword that was in the stone. I must be King. I must be King."

Sir Hector frowned. "Where did you get that sword?" he asked.

"From Arthur," said Kay, "but . . ."

He stopped. Hector was not listening. He was looking for his foster son.

The tournament was still in full swing when the three of them left for the abbey. Arthur thrust the sword back into the stone. Try as they might, neither Hector nor Kay could move it at all, but Arthur could pull it out each time at will.

Sir Hector knelt at his feet.

"Arthur, dear boy, you are my rightful King. It is a great honor to have raised you as my son. I beg a great favor in return. Please make my son, your foster brother Kay, your steward when you are crowned."

"Father, please," answered Arthur, pulling Hector up. "Whatever you ask is yours. I owe you more than I could ever repay."

The great lords were furious. Who was this upstart boy, still too young to grow a beard? Why, no one

knew who his real parents were. While they raged, Arthur stayed silent, as I had told him to. But no one else could draw that sword, while he did it with ease each time he tried.

At last it was agreed that the lords should come back at Candlemas to try the sword again. But at Candlemas nothing had changed, and they were even angrier than before. This time the decision was put off until Easter, but at Easter it was just the same. Finally, they agreed to return at Pentecost for one last try. This time even great King Agwisance of Ireland, the father of Isolde, came and took his turn, but the sword would not move for him. For the last time, Arthur stepped forward and drew the sword lightly, effortlessly out of the stone.

"It's witchcraft, sheer trickery," shouted King Clarivans of Northumberland. "The whelp's done it again."

"My lord," I answered, stepping up to Arthur's side, "we are on sacred ground. Surely you fear no witchcraft here? Come a little closer, my noble lords, and look at this young man. Look carefully at his face. Look at the features of proud Aurelius and Uther Pendragon, our late-lamented kings. Look well, for this is Arthur, Uther and Igrayne's son. This is Arthur, your rightful King."

I knelt before him as I finished speaking. A murmur ran through the crowd. It grew into a roar.

"Arthur!" the cry went up. "Long live King Arthur, long live the King!"

The next few days passed in a dream. A joyful Igrayne was reunited with her long-lost son. Bonfires lit up the sky for miles around as the good news spread that the King had come at last.

The coronation quickly followed. I sat in the abbey, next to Igrayne, as the Archbishop of Canterbury placed the precious crown upon the Boy King's head. I trembled with joy. This was the moment I had worked for, since that fateful day, long ago, on the mountainside, when the dragons fought at Dinas Emrys and my grandfather died.

WAR AND LOVE

T he new reign started well. After thirteen troubled years, Britain seemed at last to be at peace. Arthur's court flourished and, drawn by its growing reputation, knight-adventurers came from distant lands. Musicians and poets came too, and great festivals and tournaments were held. It was a time of hope.

Then, a year after the coronation, rumors seeped down from the north that Arthur's most powerful subjects, the regional British kings, were plotting a rebellion. Arthur's period of grace was clearly over. The countless hangers-on, who had infested the Boy King's court, slipped silently away. The palace at Westminster now seemed deserted.

But Arthur refused to panic. This was his first real test and he was ready to meet it. He sent out spies to find out what they could. Five anxious weeks went by when nothing was heard, but at the end of the fifth week one of the spies returned, alone. He brought bad news. Five other kings had already joined Lot, Arthur's two other brothers-in-law, Nentres and Uriens, among them. A further five kings would meet them on the march south. The rebel army already numbered sixty thousand. By the time it reached London, it would be a hundred thousand strong.

The councillors paled as they listened to the spy's report. Arthur could muster ten thousand men at most. What chance would he have against the rebel kings?

"We must get out at once, my lord," insisted Sir Kay, the steward. "We can go to Brittany, where your uncle, Duke Howel, will make us welcome. Then we can build up our strength. If we stay and fight, we're doomed."

The rest were quick to agree. There was no choice. Finally, Arthur turned to me.

"What about you, Merlin? Do we run away?"

I knew he would refuse, whatever I said. He would rather have died a hopeless, glorious death. And he was right—this was a time for courage. Besides, I had a plan.

Three nights later I was in France, visiting Uther's old allies, King Ban of Benwick and King Bors of Gaul. They agreed to come and help at once, saying that Uther's son was their son too. Within a week they had mustered twenty thousand men and we set sail for England with all haste.

A young boy sat on the rocks, watching our ships pull away from the shore. Ban, who stood on deck beside me, waved at him and the boy waved back. The boy was Lancelot, Ban's son, and this was the first time I had seen his face. I would see it again, countless times in my dreams, the face of the greatest knight ever to walk the earth.

We reached London with no time to lose, for the rebels were already on the march. During a week of frenzied preparations, Arthur showed what a fine leader he would be. He impressed even the most hardened old campaigners by giving as much attention to his cooks and supply wagons as he did to his noble knights and their magnificent chargers. By the time the army set out, Arthur had won the hearts and minds of all his men. Every last one of them was prepared to die for the sixteen-year-old King.

We hurried north. The rebels, who already outnumbered us two to one, were encamped north of the River Trent, waiting for reinforcements. We had to get there first. And we did; the second rebel army was still two days' march away when we burst through the early morning mist. The rebels had more men, but we had the advantage of surprise.

Great deeds of arms were done that day and there were many heroes. But Arthur stood out above the rest. He went wherever the fighting was fiercest, disregarding the blood that streamed from his wounds. The young lion had something to prove.

There was dreadful slaughter that day too. Unlike the great lords and knights, the ordinary troops had no armor to protect them and by the time darkness fell, sixty thousand men were dead. Corpses lay everywhere, jumbled together in the blood-drenched mud. The lucky ones died instantly, while the mortally wounded cried out to the survivors, who stumbled among them in the fading twilight, begging to be put out of their misery.

The royal army had suffered badly, but the rebel losses were terrible. Arthur had won a great victory. In return for his pardon, the rebellious kings knelt before him and swore an oath of allegiance. In their hearts they still resented him and planned treachery but, as it turned out, they were not to trouble him again.

Within days of Arthur's triumphant return to London, he faced another crisis. News came that King Lodegraunce of Camelard had been attacked by Royns, the bandit King of North Wales. Since Lodegraunce had supported Arthur against the rebels, Arthur now marched to his defense.

I stayed behind at court, exhausted by the first campaign. To my alarm, the day after Arthur left, Morgan arrived to visit her mother Igrayne. I sensed that something was about to happen and sure enough, a few days later, she took me by the arm.

"Come with me, Lord Merlin, there's something I want to show you."

It was dark inside her room and at first I could see nothing but a small light flickering in the gloom. Then I saw that the light was playing on the surface of a crystal ball. Peering into the ball, I made out three familiar faces, far away in time: Arthur, Guinevere and Lancelot. Arthur was

gazing sadly at Guinevere. She did not return his gaze. She was looking deeply into Lancelot's azure eyes.

I rushed out of the room, with Morgan's laughter echoing behind me.

"Too late, old fool," she shouted after me, "too late."

And so it proved. The young King's reputation had gone before him. Royns fled at his approach and Arthur marched into Camelard in triumph. The moment he set eyes on Guinevere, Lodegraunce's daughter, he fell in love with her. She fell in love with Arthur too, but their love was doomed. Morgan had seen to that, and there was nothing I could do.

Arthur returned to Camelot and Morgan went back to Gore. When he told me about Guinevere, I said nothing, but the faces I had seen in Morgan's room preyed on my mind.

The following day brought more bad news. A messenger came from Brittany, reporting that a foul giant, a warlow, had ravaged the country. The warlow had slaughtered thousands, captured the duke and duchess and carried them off to his lair on Mont-Saint-Michel. Duke Howel, Arthur's uncle, now languished in a dungeon, chained to the wall like a dog, and no one knew what had happened to the duchess. The Bretons desperately needed Arthur's help.

We set out that same day with a small force and found our boat ready waiting. It was a night voyage. I sat in my cabin, staring out at the stars, while my companions slept. In the middle of the night, Arthur burst in. His nightshirt was soaked in sweat. He had been dreaming, and his words came flooding out.

"I dreamed that a dragon flew out of the north, breathing fire. Its head was bright blue, its claws and wings were gleaming gold. On a high cliff top stood a huge black bear with tangled, matted hair. It roared terribly and stank of sulfur. The dragon swooped down on the bear. They lashed and slashed each other until their blood streamed down the cliff face, staining the sea. At last the bear began to weaken, dropping its head. With a final flick of its tail, the dragon swept it over the edge of the cliff down onto the rocks below."

Arthur slumped down on my bunk. He shook his head.

"The dream scared me, Merlin. Is it bad? Oh, Merlin, you understand these things. Please tell me what to do."

I smiled at the young King. It was the first time I had seen him tremble. He knew enough to be afraid of dreams.

"My lord, you've nothing to fear. For you are the dragon, Uther

Pendragon's son. The bear is the cruel giant that you will fight and overcome."

We reached the coast at dawn. Our goal was two days' march away. Broken, abandoned homesteads littered our route. Whole villages lay deserted. The people had fled to the safety of the towns and behind their closed gates sentries kept a constant watch. When they saw us pass, they shook their heads, as if to say, "Look at those fools, marching toward grim death." But Arthur was not afraid; he was the dragon of his dream.

On the third day the magic isle of Mont-Saint-Michel came into view. We made our camp on the shore, facing the mountain which rises up from the sea, and that evening, at low tide, Arthur rode out through the shallows. Sir Kay and Sir Bedevere, the royal cup bearer, were at his side.

Once they had reached dry land, Arthur dismounted and went on alone. Before long he came across an old woman, kneeling beside a freshly dug grave. Between sobs she was groaning out a prayer for the soul of her dead mistress. The duchess's agony was over.

It had turned into a dark moonless night. As Arthur climbed on up the hill, the wind howled among the rocks, piercing his armor and the leather jerkin underneath. But it was not the cold wind which froze his blood when he came, at last, to a sheltered spot, surrounded by tall trees.

The warlow sat there, licking his foul lips, while pale young women in rags prepared his dreadful meal. They were turning spits over three blazing fires. Skewered on each spit, the butchered carcases of four small children were slowly roasting in the flames.

Arthur felt sick, but the pitiful sight filled him with fury. Brandishing his bright sword, he rushed toward the giant. The warlow leaped to his feet, grabbing hold of a huge iron club which lay on the ground beside him. He towered over Arthur, as tall as the trees, but he was too late, for the young King was already inside his defenses. Before the giant could swing his club, Arthur had slashed through a trunklike ankle, severing the foot and breaking his sword in two. Then, as the giant crashed, screaming, to the ground, Arthur hacked off his hideous head with the broken sword. The warlow's reign of terror was over.

Arthur freed Duke Howel and Brittany rejoiced. On our return to London, cheering crowds lined the streets. The Boy King was now a man. Arthur had proved himself a wise King, a fine general and a great champion, and his court now flourished more than ever. New feasts and tournaments were held and the bravest knights and the loveliest ladies came. Musicians arrived from far and wide to sing of deeds of arms and deeds of love; for now the wars were over, love was in the air and the spirit of chivalry was born.

Arthur's thoughts now turned to Guinevere. The court buzzed with the news of their romance and I alone was sad, for I alone saw tragedy ahead. I told Arthur what I had seen in Morgan's crystal ball and I explained to him what it meant. For the first and last time my son, the child of my dreams, was angry with me.

"For God's sake, Merlin, can't you see that I'm in love? I love you and respect you, you've taught me everything I know, but I must make my own decision. My heart tells me to marry Guinevere and I shall follow my heart."

Messengers were sent to Camelard, Guinevere accepted and there was nothing I could do. But I wish that I had been able to prevent what happened next.

One evening, at dinner, Arthur left the hall early to go to bed, complaining of dizziness and exhaustion. I thought nothing of it at the time, for he was always short of sleep.

The drug that Morgan had put into Arthur's wine had already done its work. When her sister, Morgause, a willing accomplice, for she had always loved Arthur, slipped into their half-brother's room, Arthur was already in a trance. Instead of Morgause, wife of King Lot of Orkney and mother of Gawain, Arthur saw Guinevere. It never occurred to him that she was two hundred miles away in Camelard. By the time Morgause left him, later that same night, a boy child had been conceived. Mordred would be his name.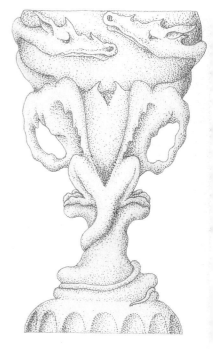

Left alone with his dreams, Arthur tossed and turned. He had a dreadful nightmare of griffons and poisonous serpents which he killed, but he was badly bitten. He ran straight for my tower on waking from his dream and, for the second time, I saw the young King tremble. As I listened to his story, the blood drained from my face.

"Arthur, Arthur, what have you done? You have lain with your sister and she has conceived a child. This is Morgan's doing, for she put her up to it. One day that child will destroy you and all your knights."

We both knew that his fate was sealed, even though the day of doom was many years away. The years of unrivaled glory were still to come.

EXCALIBUR

I knew now that my powers were fading and that my waking dream was drawing to its close. I had taught Arthur well, but I could not live his life for him; he would have to face his destiny alone. When I told him I was leaving, he begged me to change my mind, but my mind was made up. One final act remained, however. A sword had brought Arthur to the throne, but that sword had been broken. A new sword would be my parting gift.

We rode to the royal castle at Caerleon, where we fasted for three days. Then we were ready. It was a week after Morgan's treachery, just before dawn. I shook Arthur awake and he rose without a word, grabbing his cloak. Outside the stables our horses were saddled. The drawbridge was down and, apart from the faithful groom, nobody saw us leave.

We rode hard. By the time the sun came up on our right, the castle was far behind. We made our way north across the wooded plain of the meandering Usk. All through that day, we talked of government and love, of God and magic, of this world and the next; the things we had discussed a thousand times before and never would again.

We arrived at dusk. I led Arthur down to a small sheltered beach, surrounded by trees, where we tethered our horses, built a fire and made ourselves ready for the night. The moon shone brightly above us, spilling a golden pool of light in the center of the blue-black water. The lake was encircled by the soft silhouette of trees, above which the harder outline of the mountains stood against the sky. I turned to my young companion, who sat entranced.

"Years ago," I began in a low voice, "my grandfather brought me here. It was here that he told me about you. He had already had the dream, you see, and he said that one day I would bring you here to find a magic sword. Tomorrow you shall have that sword and then I shall say goodbye and take my leave forever. My work in this world is done."

The young King clasped my hand. "Dear old friend, how can I say goodbye to you? I will never forget you. As long as I live, my people will honor the name of Merlin."

That night I slept a deep and dreamless sleep. I woke to see the lake glistening beneath the rising sun while a thin veil of early morning mist still clung to the reedy banks. Arthur was standing at the water's edge, transfixed. He was staring out at the lake. I followed his gaze and saw, through the mirror-smooth surface, a slender arm, holding a gleaming sword, which reached up toward the sky.

An old boat lay hidden in the reeds, where I remembered it. We waded to it and clambered in, soaked to the waist, then we paddled out toward the sword. As we approached, we saw a woman smiling up at us through the gently rippled surface. Her black hair floated around her and her body shimmered in the water's dancing light. In her left hand was a silver scabbard, studded with precious stones.

I turned to my young companion. "Arthur, the sword is called Excalibur. It cuts through iron and steel and cannot break. Take it, it's yours."

Arthur reached out and took the shining sword. Water ran down his sleeve as he lifted it up. The blade was blue steel, hardened with secret alloys from a long-lost recipe, and the hilt was twisted ivory and gold. As we admired it, a shout of greeting echoed across the water. We looked toward the rocky island farther across the lake. The woman in the water now stood, waving at us, on a sandy beach. I smiled at Arthur's confusion.

"Don't be alarmed, she's an old friend of mine. Her name is Nynyve, the Lady of the Lake. Her magic is strong, her wisdom great."

Soon we reached the beach where Nynyve stood waiting. She was a magician of awesome power, whose knowledge exceeded even mine. She welcomed us both with a smile, and then addressed Arthur,

"My lord, I see that Excalibur pleases you. So it should; it has no match. No other mortal hand can touch it; it was made for you alone and it will serve you faithfully and well. Now I must ask you for something in return. You are still young and your reign has just begun. Years of fame and glory lie ahead. But the greatest of kings is mortal and one day you will die. When that day comes, you must return this sword to the water, the element from which it came. Otherwise the spell will be broken and the sword will tarnish and rust away. So will the memory of your name."

"As long as it is in my power," promised Arthur, "I shall do as you ask."

Then Nynyve took the silver scabbard, studded with precious stones, and handed it to Arthur. He thanked her graciously enough, but his eyes were only for the sword. I still had one last lesson to teach him.

"Arthur, you have received two precious gifts, a scabbard and a sword. Which of the two, I wonder, do you value most?"

"The sword, of course," he answered without hesitation. "The scabbard delights me. It's more beautiful than any I have seen. But in the end a simple leather sheath would do its job as well. There's only one Excalibur."

"You are mistaken," I said. "The scabbard is worth a hundred times the sword. A sword which cuts through steel and doesn't break is a fine thing, I grant you, but a scabbard protects the sword and makes it safe. And this scabbard does far more, for ancient magic made it. Not only will it sheathe your sword, it will protect your life. Nothing can hurt whoever wears it, so you should guard it as your life. And, as a King, you should always remember this: it is far more difficult to preserve life than to take it away."

"Thank you, dearest Merlin," said Arthur, clasping my hands. "And now I must go. Beyond this enchanted lake my kingdom waits. You have been more than a teacher to me, more than a friend. More, even, than the father I never knew. I shall miss you, and my country will miss your wisdom when I rule alone."

I smiled sadly. "You no longer need me, Arthur. You are ready now. Go; my old heart goes with you."

I watched the boat back to the opposite shore. Arthur untethered our horses and turned to give a final wave. Drawing Excalibur, he held it above his head. Then, turning once more, he rode off through the trees.

I went back to Nynyve, who led me to a cave under the mountains, this cave where you first met me, and who left me here dreaming in this limestone palace far beneath the troubled world.

I took to studying endlessly, poring over my books and charts, lost in a labyrinth of intricate calculations and abstract schemes. It would be many years before I realized this cave was my prison, that I was powerless to leave. Meanwhile, in dreams, I followed Arthur's life. Merlin had left the stage, but Arthur the King lived on.

THE FELLOWSHIP
OF THE ROUND TABLE

Now Arthur was alone. More than once, over the days and weeks that followed, he touched the sword and scabbard to make sure that they were real. The Lady of the Lake and our final parting had been no dream.

He did not have much time to miss me, for there was a kingdom to rule and a flourishing court to lead. His days were filled by government, while the nights were for feasting and dancing, poetry and song. There was also Camelot to be built, for only when Camelot was ready would he and Guinevere marry.

Camelot was to be the setting for the greatest court the world had ever known—a palace of dancing turrets surrounded by flower-filled meadows through which a winding river ran. I had drawn up the plans for Camelot myself, during my final year with Arthur. The finest masons in Britain were commissioned and five years later it was ready. The royal wedding was announced for Midsummer's Day and there were to be joyous celebrations throughout the land.

Soon rich pavilions, decorated with bright flags and pennants, sprang up in the meadows of Camelot. The most accomplished knights in all the world had come, the loveliest ladies too. The wedding feast would last for seven days and each day a tournament would be held.

On Midsummer's Eve, Guinevere herself arrived. She made the last stage of her journey to Camelot on a ceremonial barge which Arthur sent to meet her. A huge crowd had gathered and the sound of cheers and laughter filled the air as Arthur helped his bride-to-be ashore. Here was a royal romance indeed, a dream of love that everyone could share.

Moreover, the beautiful bride had not come empty-handed; she brought her dowry with her on an enormous wagon. This was a great round table which had been made for Uther many years before. After her husband's death, Igrayne had sent it to Camelard for safe keeping. Now Guinevere's father, Lodegraunce, was returning it to Uther's son.

The table was carried into the great hall of the palace, where Arthur ran his hand over the polished oak and gazed at the finely carved seats, depicting scenes of tournaments, hunting, noble life and love.

"I should have come alone," said Guinevere. "My lord seems to love this table more than me."

Everyone laughed, including the blushing King. Yet Guinevere's words would only too soon prove true.

The following morning, before the wedding ceremony, the Fellowship of the Round Table was proclaimed. From the moment he set eyes on the table, Arthur had thought of nothing but his idea of a great order of chivalry. At the Round Table, everyone would be equal and the best knights in all the world would win their immortal places there.

By midday the cathedral was packed. All the British kings and great British lords had come. The kings of Aragon, Castile, Cyprus, France, Naples, Navarre and Sicily came too. Saracens stood beside Scandinavians, the Emperor and Empress of Byzantium stood next to the Duke and Duchess of Burgundy. No gathering, before or since, has equaled it in splendor.

All eyes were on the royal couple. When they turned to walk slowly back down the aisle, a murmur of admiration filled the church. Arthur and Guinevere looked royal indeed. It was, said the Archbishop, a marriage made in heaven, and everyone agreed.

The King and Queen walked arm-in-arm down to the flower-filled meadows. Cheering crowds thronged their path, held back by the outstretched spears of men-at-arms who lined the route. Now and then a daring subject would dodge between the spears to kiss a royal hem.

Arthur took his place by Guinevere in the royal stand. The crowd was noisy and excited. Crushed together in the popular enclosures, people were jostling and straining to see the colors of the first knights to enter the lists. It was difficult to hear the heralds shouting out their names.

Soon all was clear; one was Sir Kay, the steward, Arthur's foster brother; the other Sir Lamerok de Gales, son of the great King Pellinore of the Isles. No one liked Kay, who had become arrogant and cruel, and a chorus of "Come on, Lamerok!" quickly sprang up.

The knights' horses snorted and reared, as they faced each other at opposite ends of the field. The royal heralds in their purple livery, embroidered with golden dragons and fleurs de lys, were flushed and sweating in the midday heat. Shouts and whistles came from every side. At last, Arthur gave a signal; the shrill trumpets blew and the tournament began.

The two knights charged toward each other, each aiming his lance at the other's chest. They met in the middle of the field. Deflecting Kay's lance with his shield, Lamerok caught him squarely in the breastplate and Kay crashed to the ground, bringing a huge roar from the delighted crowd.

The first day's tournament ended at dusk. By popular acclaim, Sir Lamerok and Sir Gawain, Arthur's nephew, were champions of the day, but many other knights won praise. The standard of jousting, everyone agreed, was higher than ever before.

The wedding feast went on all through that night. The following afternoon the tournament resumed. Once more it was a great success and, as the week went by, the seats at the Round Table were quickly filled.

It was not until the sixth day that Palomides, the mighty Saracen, took the field. He was too strong for all except Gawain. Twice they charged one another, their lances shattering on their shields. The third time they met, weary from their earlier efforts, they knocked each other to the ground. In spite of their heavy armor, they struggled to their feet and drew their great swords.

They fought until their blood flowed, staining the earth around them. The huge crowd watched in silence, hardly daring to breathe. The only sounds were the clash of swords, the clangs and thuds of steel on plate armor and chain mail, and the two knights' grunts and gasps of pain.

After an hour, faint from loss of blood, they drew apart. Resting on their swords, they turned to the royal stand. Guinevere was quick to raise her hand. The fight was over and the two brave knights embraced. A deafening cheer burst out, while Gawain and Palomides, covered in blood and dust, were carried from the field.

The seventh day dawned at last. So many noble knights had proved themselves already that only a few places at the Round Table remained to be filled. The field lay open on the final afternoon. Gawain and Palomides were still resting from their wounds and there were heated arguments about who would take their place as champion. No one noticed the stranger knight until he was right in front of the royal stand. His visor was down and he carried a plain white shield. He wore no colors—nothing to say who he might be.

The crowd was silent as he spoke.

"Your Majesties, forgive me for arriving unannounced. I have come from across the sea, riding night and day to be here. Many strange adventures have delayed me. But now, since I am not quite too late, I beg your permission to enter this tournament."

"Stranger, you are welcome," answered Arthur, "but first you must tell us who you are. It is our custom here to wear our colors openly, for no knight should be ashamed of his name."

"My lord," the stranger knight replied, "let me first match myself against the best of your knights. Then, win or lose, when I have shown what I am worth, I will gladly tell you who I am."

"My lord and husband, let him have his way. And, since you cannot fight yourself, please let him fight for me. For all these other ladies have their champions to cheer, while I have none."

Arthur smiled down at Guinevere.

"My Queen has spoken. Dear knight with no name, be sure to acquit yourself well, for our royal honor is at stake."

Unfastening her golden scarf, Guinevere stepped down from the stand and tied it to her mysterious champion's wrist. He leaned down and kissed her hand. The laughing onlookers applauded this gallantry, none more so than Arthur, while the young Queen blushed.

The stranger knight now took the field. Sir Kay insisted on being the first to face him. Envious of the attention he was getting, Kay was determined to bring him down to earth.

"Come on, brave knight with no name," he shouted across the field, "let's see how well you fall."

They rushed toward each other. At the moment of impact, the stranger swayed inside Kay's lance so that it missed him completely. Taken by surprise, Kay lost his balance and tumbled to the ground. His opponent had not even touched him.

Dismayed by the crowd's raucous laughter, the steward hurried away. Then, one by one, the best knights took their turn. One by one they were unhorsed. Even Sir Lamerok could do no better than the rest.

Finally, Arthur came down to meet the new champion. Removing his helmet at last, the strange knight knelt before the King. How well I knew that face, as I looked on from far away, in my cave of dreams.

"My lord," said the knight, "my name is Lancelot du Lac. I am King Ban of Benwick's son. I have come to Camelot to be knighted and to serve at your court."

Smiling, Arthur drew Excalibur from its magic sheath and touched Lancelot lightly on the shoulder.

"Arise, Sir Lancelot, noble knight. It completes my happiness to see you

here today. I owe you great love for your father's sake, for he helped me once when I most needed help. And now I rejoice to see that his son is a prince among knights."

That evening Lancelot took his place at the Round Table. His name had appeared on an empty seat in letters of gold. It was next to the Siege Perilous, which was covered in a golden cloth. Not even Lancelot, from that day on the greatest of earthly knights, could sit in the Siege Perilous. Only one knight would ever sit there, and that would be much later, at the time of the quest for the Holy Grail.

LANCELOT,
GUINEVERE AND ELAYNE

s Camelot's reputation spread and the Knights of the Round Table grew to be loved and feared throughout the world, the name of Lancelot stood out above all the rest. And indeed it echoes loudest still.

Lancelot's adventures would fill a hundred books. It was he who killed evil Sir Tarquin, the scourge of Arthur's knights, and who freed Tintagel from the cruel giant. He rescued Sir Tristram from Castle Orgulous·and broke the evil spell of Hallewes the sorceress. Whether in fierce battle or in friendly tournament, Lancelot had no match.

From the day of his arrival in Camelot, Lancelot was Guinevere's champion. He always wore her colors and fought for her. Arthur was too busy to do this himself and it seemed only right that his best and favorite knight should serve his Queen. Soon they were spending all their time together when Lancelot was at court and, by the time they realized that they had fallen in love, it was too late to draw back. Morgan's prophecy had come true.

It was because of their doomed love affair that Lancelot disappeared for so long, after his first visit to Corbenic, where he met Elayne. The adventure began on Whitsunday, in Camelot, where everyone had gathered for a feast. The talk was all of famous escapades and old times and many happy memories were shared. Then, when the feast was almost over, an ancient hermit hobbled into the hall.

"Old man, you are welcome," said Arthur, jumping up from his seat. "Come and sit down. There is plenty left for you."

The hermit, already stooped with age, bowed to the King.

"Royal Arthur, your words do you great honor. Many lords would throw a white-haired old fool like me straight back out through the door. However, I have not come to eat earthly food. No, I have brought a message from far away."

He limped toward the Siege Perilous and kissed it.

"Noble knight," he then whispered to Lancelot, struggling to speak, "he who shall sit here is not yet born. But his star is rising in the east. One day he will come here and the quest for the Holy Grail will begin. Then this noble fellowship will be broken up forever, to be a bright memory in time to come. But the knight who sits in the Siege Perilous will win the Grail. He will heal the maimed Fisher King and then the Waste Land will flower once again."

No sooner had the old hermit spoken these strange words, than he fell to the ground with a sigh. Lancelot reached him first, but there was nothing to be done. The old man lay there, still as a stone.

They carried his body down to the flower-filled meadows, where they buried him under an ancient oak beside the river. He had left many questions behind. Who was the Fisher King and what was the Holy Grail? And where was the Waste Land? Arthur alone knew, for I had told him of these things. But he said nothing, while his knights wondered aloud.

"I must go, my lord," said Lancelot, interrupting the speculations of the rest. "For this old man's sake, I must go in search of the Fisher King."

The other knights fell silent.

"Yes, dear Lancelot, I know," replied Arthur, clasping his friend's hands. "You must go."

He turned away to gaze at the turrets of Camelot.

"We are great and glorious now," he mused, "but one day this will all be just a dream. We are flesh and blood, Lancelot; like that holy old man who lies beneath the tree, we are flesh and blood."

That night Lancelot and Guinevere slipped down to the meadows alone.

"Oh, Lancelot," whispered the Queen, "this is

no ordinary adventure. I am afraid that nothing will ever be the same. You saw the look in Arthur's eyes when you told him you were going. Please, for my sake, please don't go."

"I must go," replied Lancelot gently, "for my honor and yours and Arthur's too. Be brave, my love, be brave. Everything will be all right, I promise. I'll come back soon, you'll see."

The following day, Lancelot left Camelot alone. For seven days he rode on and it seemed that an invisible hand was guiding him. Each night he came to a hermitage where an old man would give him directions and a bed to sleep in. Otherwise he met no one on his way. His road was lonely, but Guinevere was always in his thoughts.

At last, on the eighth day, he came to a town, which lay stretched out along the banks of a river. A magnificent bridge spanned the river and a tower stood next to the bridge. As Lancelot drew closer, he saw that a large crowd had gathered around the tower. Soon he could hear groans of agony coming from inside.

It appeared that a young woman of the town had insulted Morgan le Fay and was being horribly punished. She was trapped in a tub of scalding hot water and only the best of knights could set her free. In spite of her heart-rending cries, her fellow citizens were powerless to help her.

The bars across the tower doors dissolved at Lancelot's approach. He rushed up the winding steps to find the girl alone in a steam-filled room, naked and red, like a lobster in a pot. Lifting her out, Lancelot carried her down to the waiting crowd. The tower collapsed into dust behind them.

"Good knight," said the townspeople before he could go on his way, "there is one more thing we must ask of you."

They led him into the churchyard, where they pointed out a huge black tombstone, standing apart from the rest. Lancelot approached it alone. Close to, he saw an inscription in letters of gold.

ONE DAY A LEOPARD OF ROYAL BLOOD WILL COME AND SLAY THE DRAGON
THE LEOPARD WILL FATHER A LION THAT WILL SURPASS ALL OTHER KNIGHTS

Lancelot barely had time to make the message out before the tomb began to open. A dragon thrust out its head and blew a lethal ball of flame straight at his face. Just in time, the knight flung up his shield. Ignoring the scorching pain in his left arm, he leaped forward and thrust his sword into the dragon's throat. The creature slumped back into the tomb, spurting blood instead of fire. It would trouble the town no more.

"Now I must leave you," said Lancelot when the people came up to thank him. "I have sworn to go to the court of the Fisher King."

Their faces fell when they heard his words.

"Then you must go that way," they said, pointing to a narrow pass, high in the mountains which lay across the plain. "Beyond the mountains you will come to the Waste Land of Listinois, a dreadful and desolate place. Deep within Listinois stands the Castle of Corbenic, which some call the Castle of Adventures and others the Castle Perilous. But we warn you, since the day of the dolorous stroke, no earthly knight has been to Corbenic and left alive."

Lancelot shivered. Who knew what perils awaited him at Corbenic? And how sweet was the thought of Guinevere to him now.

It was dark by the time the lonely rider reached the top of the pass and he was trembling with cold. Seeing a faint light, he rode toward it. It came from a tiny chapel. Dismounting, Lancelot peered inside, where he saw an old hermit kneeling in prayer. Lancelot went into the chapel and knelt down beside him.

"So you have come at last," said the hermit after a long interval. "You have come at last."

"Old father, were you expecting me, then?"

"Noble Lancelot, I have been expecting you since before you were even born. For I am Nacien the hermit, cousin of Pelleam, the King of Listinois. It was I who sent for you." He lit a fresh candle as the old one died away, then turned back to the knight. "Beyond these mountains, Lancelot, lies the land of Listinois. It was once the loveliest land in all the world, an enchanted flower- and fruit-filled garden whose people lived in happiness and peace. The first King of that land was Joseph of Arimathea, that same Joseph who took the body of Jesus, our Savior, down from the Cross.

"It was Joseph who used the Holy Grail, the golden chalice which Christ drank from at the Last Supper, to collect the precious blood which ran from Christ's wounds. It was he who brought the Grail to Listinois and it is his descendants who have been its keepers ever since. They are called the Fisher Kings.

"Hundreds of years later, tragedy struck. A famous knight, called Balin, came to Listinois from Uther's court in Britain. He was given a royal welcome by Pelleam, at that time Fisher King, the kindest and most Christian King alive. But Pelleam had a brother who pretended to be a saint and who was secretly as wicked as Pelleam was good.

"This evil brother would make himself invisible and prey on Pelleam's guests. So it was that, as Balin lay sleeping in the Castle of Corbenic, the brother came to slay him in the night. Sensing his presence, Balin woke to see a dagger moving toward him. But he also noticed a man's shadow, joined to the shadow of the dagger, creeping toward him across the floor. Springing up, Balin grabbed his sword, which lay beside his bed, and thrust it in the direction of his invisible enemy.

"There was a ghastly shriek of pain as the dagger clattered to the floor. Now Balin could see the would-be murderer lying dead on the ground. His sword had snapped in two and the blade was buried deep in the dead man's chest.

"In the next instant Pelleam, who had heard the dreadful cry, burst into Balin's room. Seeing his dear brother, whose true nature had always been hidden from him, lying dead at Balin's feet, he drew his own sword to avenge him. Balin dodged aside, dashed through the open door, and ran through the castle with Pelleam in pursuit.

"Eventually, he found himself at the bottom of a steep flight of steps, leading up to a chapel. A mysterious voice came from inside the chapel saying, 'Beware, Balin, do not enter here.'

"But Pelleam had reached the far end of the corridor and Balin had nowhere else to go. He rushed up the steps into the chapel, where he was dazzled by a bright white light. On the table in front of him he thought he could see a golden bowl, bathed in a fragrant mist. A lance lay across the table, its head resting on the edge of the bowl; from the tip of the lance a drop of blood hung over the bowl.

"Seizing the lance, Balin turned and drove it through the startled Pelleam's thigh. At once there was a thunderous rumbling, deep underground. The castle walls crumbled, Pelleam fainted and a fragment of flying masonry knocked Balin unconscious to the ground.

"Balin awoke to find himself alone, outside the ruined castle. His horse was tethered beside him. From inside the castle came the sound of lamentation. Sick at heart, he rode back through Listinois, which had already turned into a bleak wasteland of blight, plague and famine. But before he reached Uther's palace, he was killed by his own brother, Balan, who mistook him for someone else.

"As for Pelleam, he has never recovered from that dolorous stroke and the blood still runs from his wounded thigh. The kingdom of Listinois is now called the Waste Land, the Castle of Corbenic remains a semiruin. One day a knight will come who will take up the Grail and heal the maimed King. But that knight is not yet born. Nevertheless, you, Lancelot, must go to Corbenic, where the new Fisher King, Pelles, son of Pelleam, will make you welcome. I cannot tell you what will happen there, but it is your destiny to go. Farewell, Lancelot, until we meet again."

Morning had broken by the time Nacien finished his extraordinary tale. Lancelot thanked the white-haired hermit, said goodbye and rode down the steep slopes into Listinois.

Despite what he had been told, he was not prepared for the vision of desolation which greeted him. Bones and blackened carcasses lay everywhere. The only living animals were scrawny and covered with sores. A few misshapen people stumbled, hollow-eyed, among the shells of their ruined houses, as though disaster had struck only hours before. In the fields, which covered the huge plain, spindly stalks of corn struggled to grow among clumps of weed. Sick at heart, Lancelot forced himself to go on.

That evening he reached Corbenic at last. As he gazed on the ruins of the castle, his heart sank still farther. The tumble-down walls and caved-in roofs had not been touched. The dilapidated interior of the castle showed through gaping holes in the battlements. Lancelot could see no sign of life. The castle appeared to be deserted.

"Welcome, noble knight. You are just in time."

Startled, Lancelot twisted around to see who addressed him. A man in white robes held up a hand in greeting.

"I surprised you, forgive me. I am Pelles, the one you seek. Please come inside at once. You have had a long, hard journey."

Once inside, Lancelot's spirits rapidly revived. When he had bathed and rested, Pelles led him to the great hall where, among the shattered columns, a marvelous feast had been laid out. The food was more delicious

than any Lancelot had ever tasted and, while he ate, Pelles told many tales of Pelleam, his father, and of the history of the Grail.

When the meal was over, a white dove appeared above the table. In its beak it held a golden bowl, which gave off a heavenly aroma, sweeter than any Lancelot had ever smelled. After a few moments the dove flew away and the sweet scent faded on the air. Immediately, a beautiful young woman came toward them, carrying the same bowl in her hands. King Pelles knelt down and prayed.

"What does this mean?" asked Lancelot, as the woman took the golden bowl away. He felt strangely light-headed.

"That was the Holy Grail itself," answered Pelles. "No living knight has seen it except you. Tomorrow I will tell you more, but now you must sleep. For tomorrow you face another arduous journey back to Camelot."

Lancelot was tired, it was true. The Fisher King led him to his chamber in the heart of the ruined castle, along a corridor and up a steep flight of steps. As Lancelot lay on his bed, gazing about the room, he thought he could see the golden bowl, shrouded in mist. A lance was resting on it and from the tip of the lance a drop of blood hung over the bowl. Before the drop could fall, Lancelot was asleep.

He dreamed that Guinevere came to him. She told him that she had found a way of leaving Camelot so that they could be together. Lancelot's dreams were sweet. In the morning, however, he woke to find not Guinevere lying beside him, but the lovely young woman who had carried the Grail the night before.

Leaping out of bed, Lancelot grabbed his sword. Before he could strike her, she opened her eyes and spoke.

"No, Lancelot, you will only harm yourself if you try to strike me here. I am Elayne, daughter of Pelles, the Fisher King. What I have done I had to do. Last night, while you were dreaming, we made a child; that child will be the perfect knight who will heal my maimed grandfather, Pelleam, and make the Waste Land blossom."

"What she says is true."

Pelles was standing in the doorway, watching them.

"Dear Lancelot," he went on, "I know that you love Guinevere alone. She is Arthur's wife, not yours, and because of that you can never receive the Grail yourself. Now your son will; one day he will return to Corbenic and heal my dear father."

On his return to Camelot, Lancelot was given a hero's welcome. The

King and Queen, especially, were overjoyed to see him back and everyone marveled to hear of his adventures. But of the Fisher King's daughter, Elayne, Lancelot said nothing. He tried to forget all about her.

However, Lancelot's cousin, Bors, was fascinated by his magical account of the journey to Corbenic. This young man was one of the Round Table's finest and bravest knights and he was determined to follow in his famous cousin's footsteps. He decided to visit the Fisher King himself.

It was about a year later that Bors, without a word to anyone, set out from Camelot alone. After two weeks, he arrived at Corbenic. A heavenly feast awaited him. Bors was ravenous after his journey and the sight and smell of the food filled him with joy. But before a single morsel had passed his lips, he found himself staring, transfixed, at the lovely young princess and the baby sleeping at her breast.

"Forgive me," he blurted out, blushing, "but your child reminds me of my famous cousin, Lancelot du Lac."

"And no wonder," replied Elayne, smiling sadly, "for Lancelot is his father."

Then Bors heard everything; how Lancelot had been tricked and how one day this child would return to Corbenic, heal the maimed King and make the Waste Land whole. No sooner had Pelles finished than the white dove flew over the table. It carried the golden bowl in its mouth, trailing a heavenly scent.

That night Bors met with many strange adventures in his dreams. The following day Pelles said goodbye to his young guest.

"Farewell, Sir Bors, farewell. One day you will return, when this small baby is a man. Then, I promise you, you will see all the mysteries of the Holy Grail."

On his return to Camelot, Bors did not mention the child until he was alone with Lancelot. The great knight embraced his young cousin and swore him to secrecy. Neither of them noticed Gawain's brother Agravain slip out from the corner where he had been hiding. He had overheard everything and went straight to the Queen.

"How could you?" hissed Guinevere when Lancelot came to her room. "How could you betray me after everything you said?"

She would not listen to Lancelot's explanation.

"Get out," she screamed, "get out, and never look at me again."

Lancelot was desperate. He loved Guinevere more than his life. He wanted to kill himself, for life without her was unimaginable. It was as though she had cast a spell on him. But he could not kill himself and bring endless shame on Arthur and the noble Fellowship of the Round Table.

He left that same night. For days he wandered aimlessly, through the forest and open country, weighed down by sorrow. Forgetting who he was became his only peace.

Camelot mourned his loss, shocked by his unexpected and mysterious disappearance. Arthur was distraught. He did not care what anyone said about Lancelot and the Queen, but he cared deeply that his favorite knight, the flower of chivalry, had gone. As for Guinevere, she was sick with sorrow and bitterly regretted her jealous anger.

The search for Lancelot went on for months. There were occasional, extraordinary reports that he had been sighted, naked and wild, deep in the forest or high on a distant crag. But even if such unlikely reports were true, no one ever got close to him. Then a year went by and there were no more sightings. Lancelot had disappeared.

HOMECOMING

I t was not long after Lancelot's disappearance that a young knight came to Camelot from Wales. This was Perceval, whose name appeared in letters of gold on the seat to the right of the Siege Perilous, next to Sir Bors. Arthur warmed to Perceval at once and Lancelot's cousin, Bors, became his constant companion.

There was another important new arrival, of a very different kind. The appearance of Arthur's son, Mordred, accompanied by Morgan, his aunt, sent ripples of alarm through Camelot. But it soon seemed that everyone's fears were groundless. Mordred was courteous and brave, while Morgan appeared anxious to patch up old differences. At her request, Arthur and Guinevere, who had no children of their own, adopted the young prince as Arthur's heir. There was no sign then of what was to come, of how treacherous the young prince would be.

Lancelot, meanwhile, had wandered far away. For three long years his home was the dense forest beyond the Waste Land, close by Corbenic. He lived on roots and berries, and the birds and wild animals were his only companions. As for his past life, he had forgotten everything: Benwick, Camelot, Arthur, Guinevere, even his own name.

One day, as he wandered among the trees, he stumbled across a wild boar, rooting for truffles in its favorite spot. Furious at being disturbed with its hoard of precious food, the boar rushed at Lancelot, and drove its gleaming tusks deep into his thigh. Despite his shock, Lancelot drew the sword that was rusting in its scabbard and cut the animal's throat. Then, faint from loss of blood, he collapsed.

An old hermit, who lived nearby, was roused from his meditations by the screeching of the birds and the choking death squeal of the boar. Dragging the half-dead Lancelot into his hovel, he dressed his wounds with ointments made up from ancient recipes. Then he wrapped them in leaves and bound them tight.

The weeks passed and Lancelot slowly recovered. As soon as he was strong enough to stand, he thanked the hermit with an inhuman grunt, for the old man was unable to heal his wounded mind, and shuffled off on his aimless way.

Lancelot's wanderings now took him out of the forest into the overgrown gardens of a ruined castle, where he lay down to sleep in the long grass by a well. He did not notice the young woman who was sitting nearby. She crept toward the sleeping knight, then jumped back in surprise. His bones showed through his meager flesh. His clothes were torn and filthy and a wild tangled beard covered his face. But the young woman trembled with recognition as she peered at him. For this was the father of her child. Lancelot had returned to Corbenic.

Kneeling beside him, Elayne gently shook him awake. He opened his eyes and looked straight through her. She spoke to him, but he did not seem to hear; he only grunted and sniffed the air. Then he turned over and drifted back to sleep.

Elayne went into the castle to fetch Pelles and her maids. Together they dragged the sleeping knight inside. They took him to the chapel and laid him before the Grail.

When Lancelot woke next day, he remembered everything. He told Elayne and Pelles how Guinevere had banished him and how, in his despair, he had gone mad. He said he could never go back to Camelot now. He would never sit at the Round Table again.

During the years which followed, Lancelot and Elayne lived together in Castle Blayant on the Joyous Isle, far from the desolation of Listinois and far from Camelot too. Their son, Galahad, lived with them and soon became his father's squire. He watched Lancelot closely, anxious to learn all he could. He could have had no better model than his father, the greatest of earthly knights. But there were other, important lessons too, and it was the ancient hermit Nacien, his great-grandfather Pelleam's cousin, who taught them to him. These were the secrets of the Fisher Kings and the mysteries of the Holy Grail, for Galahad was to be the perfect knight who would heal the maimed King and make the Waste Land whole.

As the years went by, the Joyous Isle became a second Camelot, with Lancelot its brightest star. He won every prize at tournaments as before, but he thought it wise never to reveal his real name, so that no one at Camelot would know he was still alive.

Then, one year, Lancelot entered the tournament at Surluse. He called himself "the melancholy knight," for this was the name he went by now, in memory of his years of madness and all that he had lost. Five hundred knights were at Surluse, and in the course of a single week "the melancholy knight" defeated them all.

When Gawain and his brothers returned to Camelot from the tournament, they astonished the court with their reports of "the melancholy knight," and Arthur was fascinated by their story.

"I want you to go to the Joyous Isle," he told Perceval and Ector de Marys the following day. "I want you to find out all you can about this so-called 'melancholy knight.'"

They rode for fifteen days before the Joyous Isle and Castle Blayant came into view. On the shore of the surrounding lake a boat was waiting to ferry them across. When they reached the island, a dwarf came out of the castle to greet them.

"Noble knights," said the dwarf, "you must leave your arms and your armor with me before you go inside. Unless you wish to joust with the lord of the castle first."

"We are knights errant," answered Perceval, "and we have come far to meet your lord. Nothing would make me happier than to joust with him."

"Then ring that bell," said the dwarf, pointing to the bell outside the gates, "and your wish will come true. But I warn you, you'll regret your valor when you're lying in the dust."

Ignoring the warning, Perceval approached the bell. The ringing had hardly died away when the great gates of the castle creaked open and "the melancholy knight" appeared. The two knights charged toward each other. Both lances found their mark and both knights went crashing to the ground. At once they drew their swords and circled each other on foot, exchanging savage blows.

After an hour, Perceval drew back.

"Dear knight," he said, resting on his sword, "you deserve your reputation. I will soon be forced to yield, but before I do, please tell me your name."

"I am called 'the melancholy knight,'" answered Lancelot. "Now tell me your name, for I have never met with a stronger knight."

"My name is Perceval de Gales and I come from Arthur's court."

Lancelot paled and his sword slipped from his hands.

"Then may God forgive me," he said, "since I have sworn never to raise my sword against a knight of the Round Table, except in tournaments. For now I will tell you that my real name is Lancelot du Lac, son of King Ban of Benwick, and I was once proud to be of your Fellowship."

"Noble Lancelot, I am honored," replied the young knight, falling to his knees. "And now I see why Arthur sent us to find you. For here is your brother, Ector, at my side."

It was a joyful reunion. Lancelot questioned the two knights ceaselessly about Arthur and his court. He loved Elayne and Galahad, but Camelot was where his heart still longed to be. As soon as he learned that Guinevere had forgiven him long ago, his mind was made up.

There was nothing Elayne could do to change it. The following day, with Perceval and his brother beside him, Lancelot sailed away from the Joyous Isle for the last time. Galahad sat on the rocky shore, watching them go.

When Lancelot came back to Camelot after so many years, it seemed that the celebrations would never end. Arthur rejoiced to see his best knight and dearest friend, and Guinevere, who had begun to seem sad and old before her time, was youthful and happy again. The King's pride in the Fellowship of the Round Table remained undimmed; and the exploits of younger knights like Bors, Gareth and Perceval won Camelot ever-increasing fame.

The year rushed by and the Feast of Pentecost approached. On the eve of the feast, as if from nowhere, a block of red marble appeared in the river at Camelot. A beautiful sword was stuck in the stone and on the blade was written in letters of gold:

ONLY THE BEST KNIGHT IN ALL THE WORLD

SHALL PULL ME FROM THIS STONE

"Go on, Lancelot," said Arthur, when the entire court was gathered on the riverbank. "This adventure must be for you."

"No, my dear lord," replied his favorite knight, "this sword is for a better knight than me."

What Lancelot would not do, no other knight would try, and the mysterious sword was left untouched. Who, everyone wondered, could it be for? Where was the knight who was better than Lancelot? Only Lancelot knew, but he said nothing. As for Arthur, he could not sleep that night. He stood at his window gazing across the meadows to the river, where the marble and the sword glistened beneath the stars.

Next day the court gathered for the feast. As the knights and ladies were taking their places, the doors and windows suddenly slammed shut and darkness covered the hall. Then an old man entered, accompanied by a young knight who wore an empty scabbard at his side. They stood in a silver pool of light.

Without a word, the old man led the young knight to the Siege Perilous and lifted the golden cloth which covered it. Underneath, the letters of gold gleamed out:

THIS IS THE SEAT OF GALAHAD THE PERFECT KNIGHT

The young knight sat down and turned to his companion.

"Thank you, Nacien, thank you a thousand times, old friend."

The ancient hermit bowed. "Goodbye, Galahad. I will see you once more. I must go back to Corbenic now and tell King Pelles that it is done."

The windows and doors swung open as the old man left the hall. All eyes were now on Galahad, who turned to Lancelot beside him.

"Dear father, now you must present me to the King. Then I shall get my sword from the river stone. My scabbard is empty, as you see."

Arthur led Galahad down to the river. The whole court followed and watched in amazement as, stretching out from the bank, the young knight drew the sword easily from the stone. He handed it to Arthur and knelt before him. The King knighted him as he had knighted his father before him.

That evening a sound like thunder filled the palace and darkness once again engulfed the hall. Bathed in a silvery mist, a white dove flew over the Round Table, carrying in its beak a golden bowl. From the bowl, which the knights could barely see, came a heavenly fragrance. On the table in front of them appeared the most sumptuous food that they had ever seen or tasted. Then a mysterious voice came out of the darkness, saying:

"I am the Holy Grail, the thing all holy knights must seek. Only the best may find me. Finally the perfect knight will take me and heal the maimed King, making the Waste Land whole."

"I will go," said Gawain, as the voice fell silent and the vision faded. "For a year and a day, I will go in search of honor on this holy quest."

One by one, each knight swore the same.

"Then go with my blessing, since it must be so," said Arthur in a trembling voice. "But it makes me weep to think of it, for I'm sure that many of us will never meet again."

Next day the one hundred and fifty knights of the Round Table rode out of Camelot together. That night they made camp in the forest south of Camelot. When dawn came, they rode away singly or in twos and threes in search of the Holy Grail.

For the first time since the Fellowship began, the Round Table was empty. With the knights gone, many of their ladies withdrew to their own domains, and the army of courtiers dwindled. Guinevere shut herself away for days at a time, and on many an evening the only sound in the palace was the footsteps of the lonely King, echoing in the empty halls.

THE HOLY GRAIL

A year after the departure, the first of the knights began to trickle home. They had traveled far and wide, yet none of them had found the Holy Grail.

Arthur welcomed each of them like a father welcoming a long-lost son, but his joy turned to sorrow when it became clear that for every knight who returned, another had perished in the quest. Within a month of the first arrivals, seventy knights had straggled home. A further seventy-five were known to have died and only five were unaccounted for. Despite these heavy losses, there was still no news of the Holy Grail itself and it seemed to Arthur that his knights had died in vain.

Then his nephew, Gawain, returned. The proud knight of a year before now walked barefoot, on feet that were blistered and sore. After six months of futile searching, he had met Nacien, who taught him to repent the proud and violent past which made him unfit for the quest. For the next six months, Gawain had lived like a hermit himself, praying, fasting and weeping for his sins. Finally, he had been allowed a glimpse of the Grail, at a distance, in a dream.

Not long after Gawain, Lancelot appeared with a marvelous tale to tell. He had met Nacien at the beginning of his quest and repented of his sins. He had confessed to his secret love for Guinevere and sworn, thenceforth, to be true to his God and King. So, for six months, Lancelot wore a hair shirt next to his skin and ate no meat and drank no wine. Then he took the road to Corbenic once more.

When he arrived, the castle appeared deserted. Removing his armor and laying down his sword, Lancelot went inside. No one came to greet him as he made his way across the wide courtyard, surrounded by crumbling battlements, toward the dilapidated interior of the castle. He paused at the foot of the steps leading up to the chapel. The sound of heavenly music came from inside and he sensed the sweet fragrance of the Grail. With a shout of joy, he rushed up the steps.

To his dismay, he found that the door was locked. Try as he might, he was unable to turn the handle. Meanwhile, the call of the music and the sweet scent became impossible to bear.

"Dear Lord, forgive me," cried Lancelot, falling to his knees. "Forgive me and pity me, for it would break my heart not to see the holy vision that I seek."

Even as he spoke, the chapel door flew open. The brilliant light within dazzled his eyes. As they slowly adjusted, he was able to make out the golden bowl and bleeding lance standing on a silver table, surrounded by a choir of angels.

Then Lancelot heard a mysterious voice, forbidding him to enter. But the pull of the heavenly vision was too strong and, crossing the threshold, he was engulfed in flames.

"You have seen more deeply than any living knight," said Pelles when Lancelot opened his eyes to find that the vision had gone. "Only Bors will see more and return to tell the tale. Now you must go."

One month later, Bors himself returned and the whole of Camelot gathered to hear his tale.

"We arrived at Corbenic together, Galahad, Perceval and myself. Pelles and Elaiazar, his son, came to greet us. They were overjoyed to see us and Pelles kept saying that the time had come.

"First they led us into the hall, where a large company had assembled and a great feast had been laid out. The food had an indescribable savor and the holy dove flew over us, with the golden bowl. When we had eaten, Elaiazar held up the hilt and blade of a broken sword.

"'This was the sword of Balin le Sauvage,' he told us, handing me the pieces. 'The sword which maimed my grandfather, our old King. One of you three will mend it.'

"I could see no way to repair it without a forge, so I passed it to Perceval. He handed it to Galahad in turn. To our astonishment, Lancelot's royal son simply held the pieces together and the sword was as good as new. He passed it to me, saying that I would need it more than him. Then, after the mending of the sword, came another mending. Four angels carried a bed into the hall; on it an old man lay moaning. It was Pelleam, the maimed King.

"The bed was set down before us. Immediately more angels appeared, holding a silver table, on which stood the golden bowl and the holy lance. The lance was slowly bleeding; every few minutes a drop would form on its tip and drip into the bowl.

"As the rest of us sat watching, Galahad went over to the table, took the bleeding lance and held it to Pelleam's wounded thigh. The blood dripped from the lance into his ancient wound, healing it straightaway.

"The old King leaped up from the bed where he had lain in agony for years. The castle itself was suddenly made whole, as though the ruins had never been. And from the Waste Land beyond the walls came birdsongs such as I had never heard, a dawn chorus to awaken time.

"After that we saw marvels beyond words. Our Lord Jesus Christ appeared and fed us from the Grail. It seemed that our visions would last forever.

"However, at long last they ended. Pelles now led us up to the ramparts which looked out over Listinois. Where the Waste Land had been, there was fruitful abundance now. Fields of golden corn covered the vast plain. Rivers, orchards and prosperous farms were dotted everywhere. Sleek cattle and fleecy sheep grazed in the meadows. The people were fine-looking and bright-eyed.

"To the east of the castle a vast ocean had appeared and a lovely three-sailed ship was anchored by the shore. A beautiful woman stood on the deck. Her voice floated up to us.

"'I am Nynyve, Lady of the Lake, Queen of the Waste Land, wife of Pelles, the Fisher King. Galahad and Perceval, this ship has come for you. It will carry you to Avalon, far from these earthly shores. Your work in this world is done. You, Bors, must wait a little longer. Go back to Camelot and tell them what you have seen. And pray that this story will turn their minds to God.'

"Then I accompanied my two friends down to the shore. We embraced for the last time and I cried as I watched them go. At last the ship disappeared over the horizon of this world. I said goodbye to Pelleam and Pelles, the joyful Fisher Kings, before riding back across the Waste Land, which was so fruitful now, with my heart set once more on Camelot and those I love."

Bors had finished and Lancelot, his cousin, stepped forward to embrace him.

"Dear Bors, welcome home again," said Arthur. "As you can see, many of your comrades have died. Let us honor the memory of those who lost their lives in the quest, as we honor those who achieved it."

A murmur of agreement ran round the hall.

"To the dear departed!" said the King, raising his glass.

"To the dear departed!" came the response.

Camelot gradually recovered from its heavy losses. To Arthur's delight, young knights like Florence and Lovel, Gawain's sons, and the noble brothers, Lucan and Bedevere, began to fill the Round Table's empty places. Meanwhile, however, in spite of his vows and good intentions, Lancelot began to visit Guinevere again. The lovers struggled against their desires but they were unable to stay apart for very long, and so it was that Camelot's fate was sealed.

It was Mordred and Agravain who plotted the lovers' downfall. Agravain, a mediocre knight, had always been jealous of Lancelot's glory; Prince Mordred had more sinister motives. He wanted his father's crown and he did not want to wait until Arthur died a natural death. If he could set Arthur and Lancelot against each other, the Fellowship of the Round Table would be torn apart. It would then be much easier to get rid of Arthur.

Mordred and Agravain accused the lovers in open court.

"My lord and father," said Mordred to Arthur, "open your eyes. Everyone knows what's going on but you."

Arthur frowned. He had hoped that the recent troubles were over. This sounded like more bad news. The other knights who were present had fallen silent.

"My lord and uncle," said Agravain, "Lancelot and the Queen are together all the time. People are starting to talk. Courtiers snigger behind your back. Uncle, your Queen has betrayed you with Lancelot. They must be punished."

Gawain stepped forward before Arthur could reply. Agravain was his brother, Mordred his half-brother. He was shaking with rage.

"I'm ashamed of you both," he growled. "These are foul slanders. Have you forgotten that Lancelot rescued you both from certain death when Tarquin had captured you? Yet here you are, telling stories about him to our King. I refuse to stay and listen to another word."

And bowing to Arthur, Gawain stormed out of the room. His other brothers, Gareth and Gaherys, went with him. But Agravain and Mordred were not going to back down now.

"I can understand why our brother is upset," said Mordred after he had gone. "This is upsetting for us all. But the time has come to face it. Otherwise, as Agravain has said, the scandal will spread."

Arthur walked across to the window and gazed out over the meadows of Camelot. He gripped the window ledge to steady himself; his knees felt weak and his heart was pounding. Something he had always chosen to ignore had now been dragged into the open. There would have to be an investigation. If the accusation proved true, then his Queen and his favorite would be put to death.

"My lord," said Mordred, taking Arthur's arm, "let's settle this business once and for all. It's no good accusing Lancelot openly. He would challenge us to prove it in combat and we all know he's too strong for any other knight. No, we must have proof. We must catch them together so that there can be no doubt. And when we've caught them, we'll bring Lancelot here, dead or alive, so that you can be his judge."

Arthur had no choice but to agree. That very evening Mordred had a message sent to Lancelot, saying that Guinevere wished to see him. Not suspecting treachery, Lancelot went to her rooms.

Seconds after he entered, there was a hammering at the door.

"Lancelot, come out! We know you're in there!" shouted Agravain. "If you don't come out, we'll come in and get you. And don't think about escape. There are fourteen of us out here."

The situation looked hopeless. Lancelot was unarmed. If he tried to break out, he would probably be killed. If he gave himself up, no one would believe that he and Guinevere were innocent. He would be beheaded and the Queen would be burned at the stake.

The knights began to batter at the door.

"All right," shouted Lancelot. "Calm down, my friends, I'm going to let you in." As the first knight rushed in, he slammed the door shut behind him. Before the knight realized what was happening, a heavy stool caught him in the back of the neck and he crumpled to the floor.

The battering at the door grew louder and the hinges started to give as Guinevere helped Lancelot into the dead knight's armor. Moments later a stream of fully armed knights poured into the room. By the time they realized that Lancelot was hidden by the entrance, it was too late. Only Agravain, Lovel and Florence stood between him and freedom. He hacked his way past them, killing all three, and fled.

The following morning Guinevere was taken before the King.

"We caught them red-handed and red-faced," said Mordred. "If Agravain and Gawain's milksop sons had had their wits about them, Lancelot would never have got away."

"You're a viper, Mordred," burst out Gawain, "and I don't trust you an inch. If Lancelot killed my sons, they should never have gotten in his way.

They never would have if you had not led them there. As for Agravain, he was a fool."

Gawain paused and turned to Arthur.

"Uncle, I beg you, don't be too hasty now. If you send your Queen to her death, you'll never forgive yourself. And if Lancelot were here, she would not die."

"That may well be," answered Arthur. "But a King cannot go above the law. Guinevere is guilty of treason and she must be burned."

The King's eyes watered as he spoke. He could not look at Guinevere. He forced himself to go on, holding up a hand to stop her, when she tried to speak.

"Gawain, my most trusted knight, I charge you to bring Queen Guinevere to the stake."

But Gawain refused. "If you go ahead with this, my lord, I will not be there to see it. It would break my heart to see Guinevere die."

"It will break mine too," said the King. "It will break mine too."

He turned to Gareth and Gaherys.

"Since your brother refuses to obey me, I order you to act in his place."

"My lord," answered Gareth, "we are too young to disobey like him. But we shall go unarmed and bareheaded; we will not act as jailers to our Queen."

"You may go as you wish," snapped Arthur, "but do it straightaway."

"My lord, I beg you, please . . ." It was the second time Guinevere had asked to be heard.

"You will tell the Queen that I cannot hear her," said Arthur in a trembling voice. "Please tell her to pray for her soul and that I will pray for her too."

Guinevere did not try to speak again. She turned away from Arthur and, with her head held high, allowed Gareth and Gaherys to escort her from the hall. Arthur retired to his rooms to weep alone.

Outside the palace a stake had been prepared. A large crowd had gathered around it. The royal priest was standing beside it, next to a soldier who held a burning torch. Guinevere began to shake as she was lashed to the stake. It was a horrible way to die.

The rescue was sudden and swift. Just as the flames licked up around Guinevere's feet and everyone was transfixed by the sight, six knights on horseback burst into the courtyard. Five of them held back the royal guard while the sixth forced his way up to the stake and cut the Queen free. Bystanders were trampled and cut down, Gareth and Gaherys among them, for Lancelot did not recognize them in his haste. As he galloped away, with Guinevere's arms around his waist, Gawain's two brothers lay among the dead.

The rescue party made straight for the coast. Accompanied by Bors and a handful of trusted friends, Lancelot and Guinevere set sail for France. They would go to Benwick, Lancelot's home, and wait for the storm to pass. Arthur would surely be grateful that Guinevere had been saved, when time cooled his anger and healed his wounded heart.

THE VENGEANCE OF GAWAIN

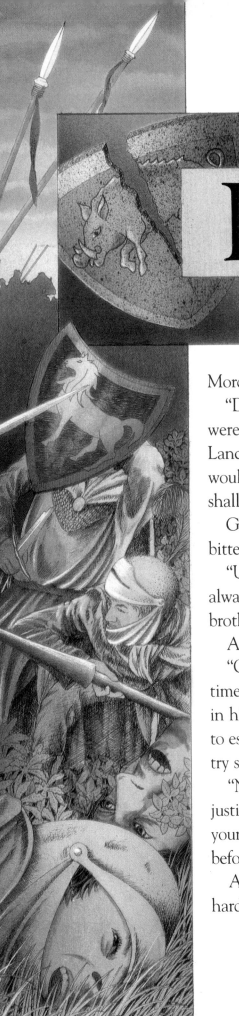

In spite of his anger, Arthur had never wanted Guinevere to die. He had condemned her to death because he had no choice; a King, like his subjects, must obey the law. When Mordred came with the news of her escape, a wave of relief washed over him. He felt that not just Guinevere, but Camelot itself, had been granted a last-minute reprieve.

The feeling was short-lived. Gawain followed hard on Mordred's heels. He was a changed man.

"Dead, both dead," he said in a voice that was flat with shock. "They were both unarmed and he slaughtered them like animals. Gareth loved Lancelot more than his own brothers and he loved us well enough. He would have helped him, not stood in his way, yet Lancelot cut him down. I shall never forgive him."

Gawain paused, looking Arthur in the eye. The King was dreading the bitter words that followed.

"Uncle, Lancelot has always been your favorite. I know that. I have always loved him too. But now I shall learn to hate him, for my dead brothers' sakes. Uncle, their deaths must be avenged."

Arthur clasped Gawain's shoulders.

"Gawain, Gawain, how could he have known? There can't have been time to see who was and wasn't armed. It was just bad luck that they were in his way. You might as well blame me. After all, I ordered your brothers to escort the Queen to the stake; I should have known that Lancelot would try something like this."

"No, uncle, my mind is made up. My brothers were murdered and I want justice. As my liege lord, I require you to hunt down the murderer. You yourself said that a King cannot go above the law. And I swear this now, before God and my King, I shall not rest until Lancelot is dead."

Arthur sighed. "Then I see that I have no choice. Lancelot will not be hard to find. He's taken Guinevere to Benwick. But, Gawain, I beg you to think again. You and Lancelot are such old friends. If you go against him now, it will mean the end of the Fellowship and everything I have built."

"There's nothing to think about," answered Gawain. "Let's not waste time. Besides, what is our Fellowship worth, when knights murder and betray each other? It has become a fellowship of shame."

Five knights of the Round Table, including Sir Bors, had gone to Benwick with Lancelot and the Queen. When Arthur announced an expedition to bring Lancelot to justice, half the remaining knights of the Fellowship crossed the sea to fight for the other side. This was just what Arthur had feared. The Fellowship was split down the middle, with loyal friends set against each other. The glorious dream that was Camelot was about to dissolve in bitterness and death.

Bullied and badgered by Gawain, whose only thought was revenge, Arthur reluctantly prepared. He appointed the treacherous Prince Mordred to govern in his absence and crossed over to France with a large army. After a week's march, they arrived at the castle of Joyous Guard in Benwick. As Arthur gazed at the towering battlements for the first time, a messenger came out to greet him. He was told that if he came in a spirit of peace and reconciliation then Lancelot would welcome him, return his Queen and kneel before him to receive his royal pardon. But if, as the presence of such a huge army suggested, Arthur had come to make war, then Lancelot begged him to change his mind.

"Go back to your master," growled Gawain before Arthur could reply to the messenger's courteous words. "Go back and tell him that his King has not come to pardon him but to see that justice is done. Tell Lancelot to come out at once to defend his honor. If he won't, then we shall have to wait and we'll wait for as long as we have to."

So the siege of Joyous Guard began. The two armies watched each other from either side of its thick, high walls. Every day Gawain rode up to the gates to challenge Lancelot to fight and every day Lancelot refused. The longer the siege lasted, the more frustrated Lancelot's followers became. They listened to Gawain's taunts and day by day their anger grew, until they could stand it no longer.

"Noble Lancelot," said Bors, who was chosen to put their case, "we know that it's love, not fear, which stops you answering insults with your sword. And for love of you we have borne with you all this time. But we can bear it no longer and tomorrow we will fight. Whether you fight with us is up to you." The moment had come at last. Lancelot could not let his loyal friends defend his honor, while he himself sat safe within his castle walls. Like his reluctant King, it seemed he had no choice.

That night Lancelot sent a message to Arthur. He would lead his men into battle the following day. He asked Arthur to forgive Guinevere and give her safe conduct home; this quarrel no longer concerned her and he, Lancelot, was proud to have rescued her from an unjust death.

With tears in his eyes, Arthur sent back his answer. He would gladly welcome his Queen, whom he had long ago forgiven. At the same time he would, sadly, prepare to fight.

Lancelot and Guinevere said goodbye for the last time. Whatever the outcome of the next day's battle they knew that, in this life at least, they would not meet again. They embraced in silence; there was nothing left to say. And what could Arthur and Guinevere say when they were reunited? What joy could there be when tragedy lay ahead? They could only cling to each other, sharing their sorrow, and forgive what they both had to forgive.

It was still dark, but the horses were saddled and ready. Guinevere's small escort, led by Lucan, expected to reach England within the week. It bothered Arthur that there had been no word from Mordred in the six months since they had left. His son had promised to send news.

"Be careful," he said, taking Guinevere's hand. "I may have trusted Mordred more than I should."

"Don't worry about me," she answered, smiling sadly. "I'm not about to fight a pointless battle, or die in the name of a justice that should be called revenge. Oh, Arthur, Arthur, why don't you come back to Camelot with me? Let Gawain and Lancelot fight it out alone."

"If only the law were as sensible as you," laughed Arthur bitterly. "Gawain is right in law and he insists that I support him."

The Queen and her escort rode off into the morning light. Soon after dawn, the two armies took the field. It was a strange battle. Friends found themselves face-to-face, while their two leaders were reluctant to fight at all. But Gawain fought savagely, looking for Lancelot everywhere, and there were plenty of knights with scores to settle after the long siege. During the months of waiting, taunts and accusations had flown in both directions across the mighty battlements of Joyous Guard. Sharp steel would answer these insults now.

Arthur rode, weeping, through the thick of the battle, unable to srike a blow. His glorious Fellowship had turned against itself and it broke his heart to see it. He would have gladly died, but it seemed that none of Lancelot's followers would raise a sword against him. He was still, after all, their beloved King.

Suddenly Arthur was cornered. A band of French foot soldiers had recognized him. Here was a rich prize indeed. They pulled him from his horse and dragged him before Lancelot.

"Say the word and we'll kill him now, my lord," cried their captain.

Lancelot angrily pushed the man aside.

"My lord, forgive me," he said to Arthur. "You know I would sooner die than hurt a single hair of your head. Now let us call a truce. I'll escort you back to your camp myself."

When he saw what was happening, Gawain was beside himself with fury. He galloped toward them, reining up his horse in their path.

"Uncle, what does this mean? You promised me justice and I hold you to your word. I'll never forgive you if you make peace with this traitor."

"Oh, Gawain," said Lancelot, "your quarrel is with me, not with the King. And I beg you to forgive me. I'll do anything to make amends."

"Lancelot," replied Gawain, "I will never forgive you. You must pay for my brothers' murder with your blood. But the battle can stop now if you'll fight with me alone."

Lancelot accepted the challenge at once, and the same knights and men-at-arms, who minutes earlier had been exchanging ferocious blows, now embraced one another as friends. Then they watched in silence as Lancelot and Gawain rode to opposite ends of the field.

They had met in tournaments many times before and Lancelot had always won. But the spirit of vengeance spurred Gawain on, while Lancelot had no heart for the fight. Gawain had special power too. Before leaving for France, he had secretly visited Morgan le Fay, his aunt, begging her to help him overcome Lancelot and avenge his brothers. She cast a spell over him so that between the hours of nine and noon his strength would treble. However, once noon had passed, it would gradually fall away and he would have to rely on himself again.

It was just after nine when the two knights charged toward each other. They met with tremendous force, each driving the other from his saddle. Their huge horses staggered aside. Gawain was up first and he rushed at Lancelot with his sword held high. Making a desperate effort, Lancelot rolled aside as Gawain's sword crashed down. By the time Gawain had recovered his balance, Lancelot was on his feet. But Gawain's ferocity surprised him. This was not the Gawain he remembered. His blows were fiercer and came far faster than before. The onlookers were astonished too. Lancelot, who had never been defeated, in tournament or battle, was struggling to survive.

But midday came and Lancelot was still on his feet. Just when he felt he could hold out no longer, he sensed his opponent weaken. Gawain was still dangerous, but the tide had turned and Lancelot was soon matching him blow for blow. Gawain launched one final, desperate attack and found himself sprawling on the ground, Lancelot's sword at his throat.

"Forgive me and forget this hatred," Lancelot cried.

"Never! Kill me, or I'll fight you again as soon as my wounds are healed."

"Gawain, I'm sorry that your heart is set so hard against me, but I've never killed a fallen knight and I won't start now." So saying, Lancelot left him and went back to Joyous Guard.

Gawain was carried to the royal camp, where his wounds were staunched and bandaged. Since Lancelot had won, Arthur insisted on giving him a royal pardon. If Gawain chose to oppose it, he would then be outside the law. But the crisis never came. Before Gawain had recovered, news arrived from England at last. And the news was very bad.

t was past midnight when Lucan reached Arthur's camp at Joyous Guard. He was shivering with exhaustion and cold; he had not slept since leaving England the week before and the night frosts of early winter had begun.

"From Guinevere, my lord," said the young knight, handing the sealed letter to Arthur. The King made him sit by the fire, then snapped open the seal and started to read.

"Dearest husband, may it please God this letter reaches you safely. If only the news I send were not so bleak. When we landed in England, it was just as you had feared. Mordred's spies had informed him that we were coming and we were arrested on arrival. We were taken to London, where, to my horror, we discovered that the people had been told that you were dead and Mordred had had himself crowned King.

"Worse, if worse there could be, was to follow. Mordred told me that he had decided to marry me and make me his Queen. He said that if I refused I would die a horrible death (I will not relate the gruesome details here). I realized at once that I had to be cunning, so I pretended that I had secretly loved him since the day he first came to Camelot and that nothing could make me happier than to be his wife. Mordred was deceived and immediately announced our wedding. Then I asked for permission to go to Camelot to prepare myself and collect my clothes and jewels.

"I told Lucan my plan and we set off the following day with a party of faithful ladies-in-waiting and trusted knights. We rode straight to the Benedictine abbey at Amesbury, near Camelot, where the abbess made us welcome and gave us sanctuary.

"Mordred, of course, was furious. He descended on Amesbury with his army of mercenaries and traitors. But in spite of his entreaties and threats the abbess refused to hand me over. Even Mordred, whose power is based on bribery and terror, did not dare break into such a holy place. Instead, he shouted horrible curses and threats before riding away. Hours later, clouds of thick black smoke billowed up into the sky from the direction of Camelot. I knew that your son had taken his spiteful revenge.

"My lord and dearest husband, I pray this letter reaches you. Gawain's vengeance must be forgotten now. Your country needs you as never before. The people dread a return to the bad old days of Vortigern. Come back at once and set them free."

"My lord?" said Gawain softly. He had watched Arthur's face whiten as he read the letter. Arthur handed it to him without a word.

Within a day the army was ready to march. Before leaving, Arthur visited Joyous Guard. Lancelot begged to be allowed to come to England and fight but Arthur said no. Gawain's wounds were almost healed, but his heart was still sore. They must let time do its work. So Arthur and Lancelot said goodbye.

Mordred's spies had been busy. The usurper was waiting with a large army and he attacked his father's troops as they were landing. Arthur fought as though he were young again. The lion of England led his men forward and, although they were heavily outnumbered, they fought so fiercely that Mordred's army was scattered in all directions.

Arthur had won a glorious victory. If only Lancelot had been there too, the rebellion would have been shattered beyond repair. As it was, Mordred's supporters were able to regroup.

The victory was spoiled by sorrow too. Gawain, whose wounds had not fully healed, insisted on fighting. Now he lay dying in the field.

"Dear uncle," he whispered when Arthur was brought to him, "I die in sorrow, for I have brought this about. Because of my pride your kingdom lies in ruins. If not for me, Mordred would never have seized your throne. I

beg you one last thing. Have a pen and paper brought. I want to write to Lancelot before I die." A scribe was sent for. Arthur held the dying knight, as he dictated the following words: "Dearest Lancelot, I, Gawain, son of King Lot of Orkney, greet you. I lie dying of the wound you gave me, which has been reopened in battle here. I therefore claim that you have killed me, for I could not wish to die at nobler hands. I forgive you my brothers' deaths with all my heart, as I know that they would have wished me to. And I beg you, dearest friend, to come at once to England, with Bors and your fellow knights and the largest army you can muster. For my treacherous brother Mordred will destroy Arthur if he can. Forgive me, Lancelot, dearest friend, forgive me and pray for my soul." With these words, Gawain died in Arthur's arms.

A week later came the news that Mordred had raised another army in London and the surrounding counties. He had dazzled the people with promises of riches, which they had been too greedy to resist. Now he was ready to attack his father before the royal army could gather strength.

Arthur marched westward along the coast, hoping to muster support. Mordred pursued him. The King quickly realized that the farther his army marched the more exhausted it would become; so on the third evening of the march, Arthur's army pitched camp on the edge of the South Downs by the sea. The King had made up his mind. He would turn and face Mordred here.

On the eve of the battle, Arthur had a dream. He dreamed he was back in Camelot, sitting on a wonderful throne which was attached to the top of a huge wheel. Scenes of happiness and delight surrounded him. But far beneath him he saw a deep black pool where thousands of foul monsters writhed and thrashed about. As Arthur looked down at this hideous sight, the wheel began to turn. He struggled to jump clear, but found that he was stuck fast. Then, as his throne sunk lower with the turning wheel, he started to slide off. He clutched at the sides, desperate to cling on, but they slipped through his hands and he fell away, down, down toward the writhing mass in the water below.

He woke in a sweat. He did not need me to interpret this dream. Outside the first faint streaks of light were brightening the eastern skies. Arthur sensed that even his magic scabbard would not save him; the coming day would be his last.

Feeling quite calm, he drifted back into the half-sleep of another dream. Now he saw Gawain standing before him as if he was still alive.

"Dear uncle," said Gawain, "if you fight tomorrow, you will go to your death and both armies will be destroyed. Make a truce with Mordred, whatever the cost. In a month Lancelot will arrive, with a great army and the rest of your knights. Then the traitor will be destroyed."

Later that morning Arthur held a council in his tent. When they heard his dream, everyone agreed that Mordred should be persuaded to accept a truce. So Lucan and Bedevere were sent to Mordred's camp. The treacherous prince greeted them with contempt—why should he wait when he was so much stronger now? But as he listened to their offer he began to change his mind. If he agreed to a truce, he would receive a royal pardon and be confirmed as Arthur's heir. At the same time, he would be made Duke of Kent and Cornwall and Prince of Wales. The terms were too generous to refuse. At midday the two armies drew up face-to-face. White flags fluttered everywhere as father and son rode slowly toward each other.

It was an uneasy meeting. Both men had every reason to suspect a trick and their bodyguards kept their hands on the hilts of their swords. Their edginess spread to their horses, which twitched nervously, sniffing the air. The massed ranks of knights and men-at-arms watched in silence as Arthur and Mordred dismounted and embraced. Everyone held his breath, ready for treachery.

But no one was expecting a simple trick of fate. And no one realized what had actually happened until it was too late. The horses disturbed an adder which lay curled up in the long grass. Before it could strike, Lucan had drawn his sword and slashed off its head. All the onlookers saw was a flash of steel and the entire scene was immediately transformed. The white flags came down in waves and Mordred's and Arthur's colors sprang up in their place. Horns sounded, trumpets blew and drums began to roll. It was too late to stop it; the two sides had begun to fight.

The battle raged all day. The armies were so close together that everyone was trapped, and in the hand-to-hand fighting there was an enemy at everyone's back. The carnage was terrible. By nightfall Arthur found himself alone with Bedevere and Lucan, who was badly wounded; it seemed that no one else was left alive. Then Arthur saw Mordred, picking his way among the piles of corpses.

"Lucan, give me your spear, quick. He won't escape me now."

"Lord," cried the wounded knight, "remember your dream and let him be. If you live through today, you won't have to wait long for revenge."

Arthur gazed over the grim battlefield. Apart from these two and the knights who had stayed with Lancelot, none of the Fellowship survived. Camelot lay in ruins and he was too old to start again. Grabbing Lucan's spear, he rushed at his treacherous son. As he ran, his sword-belt came loose and Excalibur and the scabbard fell to the ground.

Mordred saw him coming, but too late. Arthur drove the spear through his black and envious heart. As he fell, Mordred lashed out wildly with his sword, catching the side of his father's head. Arthur staggered away from his dead son into Bedevere's arms. Together with his brother, Lucan, Bedevere carried the dying King down toward the beach. Lucan collapsed as they laid Arthur on the sand. Now only Bedevere was left. Sobbing, he held his dead brother's body.

"Bedevere," whispered the King, "there's no time to weep now. I must leave this world quickly, before I die. Fetch Excalibur and throw it into the sea. Then come straight back and tell me what you've seen."

Picking up the sword, Bedevere carried it to the water's edge. But as he stood there, looking at the hilt studded with precious stones and the marvelous scabbard hiding the blade of bright steel, he could not bring himself to throw it in. So he left it by a rock and went back to the king.

"Well," asked Arthur, "what did you see?"

"In truth, my lord, I saw nothing but waves and gulls."

"Bedevere, don't deceive me. Go back and do what I ask."

But for the second time Bedevere's courage failed him. Again he left Excalibur by the rock. Arthur was desperate now.

"Bedevere, if you betray me now, then I will die forever and you will have killed me."

At these words, Bedevere ran back to the rocks, picked up Excalibur and hurled it with all his might into the billowing waves. As he watched, an arm came out of the sea to catch it. The arm brandished the sword three times, then disappeared.

When Arthur heard what had happened, he asked Bedevere to drag him down to the water's edge. A lovely three-sailed ship was waiting there. Two women stood on the deck as Bedevere carried the king aboard.

"Welcome, Arthur," said a familiar voice. "I am Morgan le Fay, your sister, now Queen of Avalon, the magic island where we will take you to heal your wounds."

"Welcome, Arthur," said the woman beside her. "I am Nynyve, Lady of the Lake, Queen of the Waste Land, and wife of the Fisher King. I have come to take you on your last voyage."

The ship began to move and soon it was floating away from the shores of England into the mists of time. Bedevere watched it go, until it disappeared from view. Then he turned away and walked up the beach alone.

MERLIN'S FAREWELL

With Arthur's parting my story ends, this marvelous tale of long ago. Later, Lancelot would return to England, and spend his last years at Glastonbury as a monk, now truly a knight of God. After the terrible destruction of the last battle, the country slowly recovered. New kings came and went, some good, some bad, and many more noble knights were to make their names. But however much the people longed for them, the wonderful days of Arthur were never to return. I, Merlin, long for them still, imprisoned forever in my cave, where I dream of Arthur, King of Britain and Camelot, who perhaps lives to this day, far away in the enchanted land of Avalon.